# FROM THE PAGES OF *AESOP'S FABLES*

Slow and steady wins the race.
(page 114)

Pride comes before a fall.
(page 135)

Revenge is a two-edged sword.
(page 137)

A man is known by the company he keeps.
(page 173)

Think twice before you act.
(page 182)

Be content with your lot.
(page 182)

When you hit back make sure you have got
the right man.
(page 194)

Once bitten, twice shy.
(page 197)

Out of the frying pan into the fire.
(page 213)

One good turn deserves another.
(page 235)

# AESOP'S FABLES

## AESOP

*With an Introduction and Notes
by D. L. Ashliman*

*Illustrations by
Arthur Rackham*

George Stade
Consulting Editorial Director

**BARNES & NOBLE CLASSICS**
NEW YORK

JB

## BARNES & NOBLE CLASSICS

NEW YORK

Published by Barnes & Noble Books
122 Fifth Avenue
New York, NY 10011

www.barnesandnoble.com/classics

The present text of *Aesop's Fables* derives from V. S. Vernon Jones's edition published
by W. Heinemann in 1912. Spelling and punctuation have been Americanized,
printer's errors corrected, and capitalization standardized throughout.

Published in 2003 by Barnes & Noble Classics with new Introduction,
Notes, Biography, Chronology, Inspired By, Comments & Questions,
and For Further Reading.

Introduction, Notes, and For Further Reading
Copyright © 2003 by D. L. Ashliman.

Note on Aesop, The World of Aesop and His Fables,
Inspired by *Aesop's Fables*, and Comments & Questions
Copyright © 2003 by Barnes & Noble, Inc.

*Aesop's Fables*
ISBN-13: 978-1-59308-062-4
ISBN-10: 1-59308-062-X
LC Control Number 2003108022

Produced and published in conjunction with:
Fine Creative Media, Inc.
322 Eighth Avenue
New York, NY 10001

Michael J. Fine, President and Publisher

Printed in the United States of America

QM

20  22  24  26  28  30  29  27  25  23  21

# AESOP

Aesop may not be a historical figure but rather a name that refers to a group of ancient storytellers. And if a man named Aesop did exist, it is unlikely that he committed any of his immortal fables to paper. After his presumed date of death several centuries passed before the first reliably known written collection of the stories appeared. What, then, is known of this elusive author, of whose true identity, like Homer's, we have but a hazy impression?

Tradition says that around 620 B.C., Aesop was born a slave in one of the ancient city-states in Asia Minor, on the Greek island of Samos, or in Ethiopia or another locale. A man named Xanthus owned him first, and then Iadmon; because of Aesop's marvelous wit and capacious intellect, Iadmon gave him his freedom. According to Plutarch, Aesop served as a shrewd and capable emissary to the wealthy Croesus, king of Lydia, who employed the fabulist in his court, where he dined with philosophers and from which he traveled on ambassadorial missions. The brilliant storyteller reportedly journeyed throughout Greece, doing business for Croesus and delighting the citizens of many cities with his fables.

As the fables that bear his name suggest, Aesop must have been a clever and wisely observant man, but according to one account of his death, his keen sense of human behavior was his undoing. Croesus had entrusted Aesop with a fortune in gold and sent him as an emissary to Delphi, with instructions to spread the sum throughout the land. But the avarice of the citizens disgusted Aesop, and he declined to hand out the money. Sadly, his mistrust of the people was well founded, for they executed Aesop, some say by hurling him from a cliff-top.

The death of Aesop the man had little impact on the life of his works, and collections of "Aesop's fables" grew and flourished through the ages, in both written and oral form. They were among the first printed works in the vernacular European languages, and writers and thinkers throughout history have perpetuated them to such an extent that they are embraced as among the essential truths about human beings and their ways.

# TABLE OF CONTENTS

# THE WORLD OF AESOP AND

## HIS FABLES

| | |
|---|---|
| c. 2000 B.C | In ancient Mesopotamia proverbs and fables featuring animals are recorded on clay tablets. Probably based on older material, now lost, such stories were most likely invented independently in more than one place; prehistoric travelers carried them back and forth across the world. |
| c. 620 | Aesop was born a slave or possibly captured into slavery at an early age; his birthplace might have been Thrace, Phrygia, Samos, Athens, Sardis, or Ethiopia. As a young man he was taken by a slave trader to what is now Turkey. When no one would buy him, he was taken to the island of Samos, where a man said to be a philosopher called Xanthus purchased him as a servant for his wife. Later he was owned by Iadmon, a Samian, who gave Aesop his freedom. |
| Seventh–sixth centuries | The Seven Sages of Greece—Solon of Athens, Chilon of Sparta, Thales of Miletus, Bias of Priene, Cleobulus of Lindos, Pittacus of Mitylene, and Periander of Corinth—are revered as the source of the highest practical wisdom. According to Plutarch, Aesop is a guest at one of the sages' banquets. |
| c. 560 | Aesop's cunning, wisdom, and oratory had freed |

him from slavery, but this year they will cost him his life. The citizens of Delphi, offended by perceived insults to their aristocracy and the god Apollo, plant a golden cup in his baggage, then accuse him of having stolen it; they execute Aesop by throwing him off a cliff.

425     In his *History* of the Greco-Persian wars, the Greek historian Herodotus writes about Aesop.

422     In his comedy *Wasps*, Aristophanes notes that, at banquets in ancient Athens, a common entertainment was the telling of anecdotes and comic stories in the style of Aesop.

360     Plato records in his dialog *Phaedo* that Socrates, in prison awaiting execution, had diverted himself by writing some of Aesop's fables in verse.

c. 300    In Athens, Demetrius Phalareus may compile the first collection of fables attributed to Aesop, but it will not survive after about 900 A.D. In India, the first of the didactic *Jataka* tales are written and will continue to be recorded until about 400 A.D.; many are based in ancient folklore and have close parallels in Aesop. Part of the canon of sacred Buddhist literature, the collection—some 550 anecdotes and fables—depicts early incarnations of the Buddha.

c. 100    In India, a Sanskrit collection of tales is collected that will form the basis for the *Panchatantra* (see third and fourth centuries A.D.).

First century The Roman poet Horace records, in his *Satires*, one of the most famous of Aesop's fables, "The Town Mouse and the Country Mouse" (no. 141).

c. 15 B.C.  Phaedrus is born as a slave in Thrace; at a young age he moves to Italy, where he gains his freedom. He will live until 50 A.D.

First century A.D. In Rome, Phaedrus records the oldest surviving collection of Aesopic fables in Latin iambic verse; the five books of his collection contain

|                    | some 94 fables. Later editors will rely heavily on Phaedrus as a source for their "Aesop's fables." |
| Second century     | Babrius, probably a Hellenized Roman, assembles the oldest extant collection of Aesopic fables in Greek. It includes more than 200 fables, 143 of which are still extant in verse form; 57 others have survived paraphrased in prose. Babrius's Aesopic fables will also serve as a source for later editors. |
| Third–fourth centuries | In India, the *Panchatantra* is compiled; many of these 87 animal fables were ancient oral folktales. |
| 400                | Flavius Avianus rewrites in Latin verse 42 of the Greek fables from the Babrius collection. Although these stories are not as succinct as the best fables, the collection will be influential in medieval Europe and often used in schools. |
| c. 1000            | The great collection of Arabic short fiction *The 1001 Nights*, also known as *The Arabian Nights' Entertainment*, is compiled; based on Indian, Persian, and Arabic folklore, many of the individual stories are undoubtedly even older. In addition to romantic tales of fantasy and magic, *The 1001 Nights* also contains a number of Aesop-like animal fables. |
| c. 1160–1190       | Marie de France, the greatest woman author of the Middle Ages, composes 103 original fables in French verse; called *ysopets*, they are in the Aesopic tradition. |
| c. 1300            | The Byzantine scholar Planudes Maximus compiles a well-regarded collection of Aesop's fables and writes the earliest known biography of Aesop. His most likely fictional descriptions of Aesop portray him as monstrously deformed. However, ancient texts that refer to Aesop make no mention of any such deformity. |
| 1330               | The popularity of fables attributed to Aesop leads to new literary creations in the same tra- |

dition. This year, an anonymous English scribe writes *Gesta Romanorum* (Deeds of the Romans); among the 283 recorded "deeds" are a dozen animal fables similar to those of Aesop.

c. 1450    Movable-type printing is developed, greatly facilitating the publication of fable collections in vernacular languages throughout Europe.

1461       The first book printed in German is a collection of fables attributed to Aesop and Flavius Avianus; compiled by Ulrich Boner, it is titled *Der Edelstein* (The Precious Stone).

c. 1476    Heinrich Steinhöwel publishes *Esopus*, a collection of fables in Latin and German; translated into French, Italian, Spanish, Dutch, and Czech, it will become an international bestseller.

1484       William Caxton publishes an English translation of the French version of Steinhöwel's *Esopus*; it is among the first books published in English.

1668–1694  Jean de La Fontaine publishes about 240 poems in the Aesopic tradition; many readers today know Aesopic fables primarily through La Fontaine's rendition.

# INTRODUCTION

"Don't count your chickens before they are hatched!" "He is a wolf in sheep's clothing." "She has a sour-grapes attitude." "They are killing the goose that laid the golden eggs." "He demands the lion's share." "Don't be like the boy who called 'wolf!' " These expressions are so much a part of our everyday language and culture that they seem to have been with us forever, and that is almost the case, for the fables that produced these proverbial sayings are indeed even older than (to name but three) the modern English, French, and German languages where today they are so much at home. The fables behind these sayings are those of arguably the most famous storyteller of all time, the legendary Aesop. Who was the man who created these timeless literary gems?

### The Man Aesop

Aesop (sometimes spelled Æsop, Æsopus, Esop, Esope, or—using the Greek form of his name—Aisopos) has been known in history and in legend since the fifth century B.C., or earlier, as a gifted Greek storyteller and the author of the world's best-known collection of fables. However, it cannot be proven with any degree of certainty that he existed as a real person. Most modern scholars believe that Aesop was instead a name invented, already in antiquity, to provide attribution for a body of oral tales whose true authors were a number of anonymous storytellers. Martin Luther expressed this view some 500 years ago: "Attributing these stories to Aesop is, in my opinion, itself a fiction. Perhaps there has never been on earth a man by the name of Aesop" (quoted in Jacobs, *History of the Aesopic Fable*, p. 15; see "For Further Reading").

Although it is possible that there was indeed a gifted Greek storyteller by the name of Aesop, his reputation expanded to legendary proportions in the decades and centuries following his death, and with time many more stories and deeds were credited to him than he could have composed and performed. Supporting this view, many of the earliest references to the stories of Aesop refer to Aesopic (or Aesopian) fables rather than Aesop's fables. In other words, Aesopic, an adjective, describes a kind of story and a literary tradition but does not claim to identify a specific author.

One thing is certain: Aesop, if he existed at all, did not leave behind a collection of written fables. His reputation is that of an oral storyteller, not an author of written literature. The oldest references to his fables refer to tales memorized and retold, not written and read. For example, from Aristophanes' comedy *Wasps* (written in 422 B.C.) we learn that telling anecdotes and comic stories in the style of Aesop was common entertainment at banquets in ancient Athens. More seriously, in 360 B.C. Plato recorded in his dialog *Phaedo* (section 61b) that Socrates, under sentence of death in prison, diverted himself by reformulating some of Aesop's fables. Plato's Phaedo quotes Socrates himself: "I took some fables of Aesop, which I had ready at hand and knew, and turned them into verse." The doomed philosopher did not have a book or manuscript of Aesop's fables in prison with him, if such a book or manuscript even existed at the time. He knew the fables from memory, as did the partygoers in Aristophanes' comedy.

The most frequently cited ancient reference to the man Aesop is found in the *History* of the Greco-Persian Wars written by the Greek historian Herodotus about 425 B.C. Here we learn that Aesop, the fable writer, was a slave of Iadmon, son of Hephaestopolis, a Samian, and that Iadmon's grandson (also named Iadmon) claimed and received compensation for the murder of Aesop. If this account is true, Aesop would have lived during the sixth century B.C. Apart from this sketchy biography, Herodotus recorded essentially no additional details about the fable writer.

However, later Greek and Roman writers were not so reticent. One body of literature is particularly relevant in this regard. Usually referred to as *The Life of Aesop*, this work has survived in a number of medieval manuscripts by different anonymous compilers and is based on earlier accounts, now lost. The statements about Aesop's life history contained in the different versions of this work often contradict one another, or they are so miraculous and fantastic as to be unbelievable by modern standards.

The ultimate source of these accounts is undoubtedly folklore: anonymous legends told and retold by generations of oral storytellers. *The Life of Aesop* is today generally held to be fiction, but as is the case with many legends, there could be at least a kernel of truth in one or more of the episodes. The following biographical outline has been gleaned from different versions of *The Life of Aesop*, most prominently the accounts published by Lloyd W. Daly in his *Aesop without Morals* (pp. 31–90) and the *Everyman's Library* version of *Aesop: Fables* (pp. 17–45).

Aesop was born a slave, or possibly was captured into slavery at an early age. His birthplace is variously stated as Thrace, Phrygia, Ethiopia, Samos, Athens, or Sardis. He was dark-skinned. In fact, it is said that his name was derived from *Aethiop* (Ethiopian). He was physically deformed: a hunchback, pot belly, misshapen head, snub nose, and bandy legs are often mentioned. Although in his early years he suffered from a serious speech impediment, or—according to some—the inability to speak at all, he was cured through the intervention of a deity and became a gifted orator, especially skillful at incorporating fables into his speeches.

As a young man Aesop was transported by a slave trader to Ephesus (in modern Turkey). Because of his grotesque appearance, no one there would buy him, so he was taken to the island of Samos, where he was examined by Xanthus, identified in the manuscripts as "an eminent philosopher," but a person whose existence cannot be verified historically. At first repulsed by Aesop's appearance, Xanthus changed his mind when the slave proclaimed, "A philosopher should value a man for his mind, not for his body." Impressed with Aesop's astuteness, Xanthus purchased him as a manservant for his wife.

Aesop soon proved himself to be an irreverent and sarcastic trickster with a clever retort for every occasion. The following episode is typical of many others illustrating how Aesop's quick wit saved him from punishment, sometimes deserved, sometimes not. Xanthus, wanting to know what fate awaited him on a particular day, sent Aesop to see if any crows were outside the door. According to popular belief, two crows would portend good fortune, whereas a single crow would be an omen of bad luck. Aesop saw a pair of crows and reported this to his master, who then set forth with good cheer. Upon opening the door, Xanthus saw only a single crow, for one of them had flown away, and he angrily turned on his slave for having tricked him into beginning a dangerous venture. "You shall be whipped for this!" said Xanthus, and while Aesop was being readied for his punishment a messenger arrived at the door with an invitation for Xanthus to dine with his friends. "Your omens have no meaning!" cried Aesop. "I saw the auspicious pair of crows, yet I am about to be beaten like a dog, whereas you saw the ominous single crow, and you are about to make merry with your friends." Perceiving the irony and the wisdom of this observation, Xanthus released Aesop and spared him the threatened punishment.

Aesop's cleverness extended from word to deed. An unrepentant trickster, his pranks ranged from tricking his fellow slaves into carrying the heavier burdens, to seducing his master's wife with her unwitting husband's apparent blessing. His tricks often were masked by feigned stupidity on his part, which has led commentators to compare him to the German Till Eulenspiegel and the Turkish Nasreddin Hoca, two of the world's most rascally, but beloved tricksters.

Aesop's legendary wisdom and shrewdness sometimes moved into the realm of the supernatural. He could solve seemingly impossible riddles and conundrums, foretell the future with uncanny accuracy, and unerringly discover hidden treasures. A master of human psychology, he understood what motivated people to act, and used this knowledge to manipulate them to his advantage. As his life progressed he moved to ever greater venues: from a trickster in a slave's workroom to a lecturer in a philosopher's auditorium to a diplomat and councilor in the courts of governors and kings.

With time his cunning, wisdom, and oratory skills brought him freedom from slavery, but in the end they cost him his life. At Delphi the citizens, offended by his lack of respect for their aristocracy and for their principal deity Apollo, planted a golden cup in his baggage, then accused him of temple theft.

Sentenced to die by being thrown over a cliff, Aesop pleaded his case with a series of fables, one of which was the story of "The Mouse, the Frog, and the Hawk" (no. 67 in the present collection). In this tale a frog and a mouse go swimming together in a pool with their feet tied together, but the mouse drowns. The frog, burdened by the dead mouse, is now an easy prey for a hawk, which forthwith captures and devours him.

Aesop compared himself to the mouse and the Delphians to the frog. "You may kill me," he predicted, "but my unjust death will bring you great misfortune." Aesop was executed near Delphi, and his dire prediction came true. Shortly after his death the region was visited with famine, pestilence, and warfare. The Delphians consulted the Oracle of Apollo as to the source of these calamities, and they received the answer that they were to make amends for the unjust death of Aesop. Accordingly they built there a pyramid in his honor.

### Ancient Greek and Latin Collections

Unlike with later collectors, editors, and authors of tales, such as Charles Perrault, the Grimm brothers, and H. C. Andersen, it is not possible to establish an authoritative canon of stories attributable to Aesop, nor does there exist a standard version of Greek or Latin fables in the Aesopic style.

The first mentioned collection of fables attributed to Aesop is said to have been compiled in Athens by one Demetrius Phalareus about 300 B.C., but this work is no longer extant. It did not survive later than about 900 A.D., and it is not known how many stories this collection contained, nor which specific fables it included.

The oldest surviving collection of Aesopic fables was recorded in Rome in Latin iambic verse by Phaedrus during the first century A.D. Phaedrus was born as a slave about 15 B.C. in Thrace; at a young age moved to Italy, where he gained his freedom; and died about 50 A.D. Divided into five books, Phaedrus's collection contains some 94 fables. The opening lines of his prologue are instructive: "Aesop is my source. He invented the substance of these fables, but I have put them into finished form. . . . A double dowry comes with this, my little book: it moves to laughter, and by wise counsels guides the conduct of life. Should anyone choose to run it down, because trees too are vocal, not wild beasts alone, let him remember that I speak in jest of things that never happened" (Perry, *Babrius and Phaedrus*, p. 191). Later editors relied heavily on Phaedrus as a source for their "Aesop's fables."

The oldest extant collection of Aesopic fables in Greek was authored by Babrius (sometimes identified as Valerius Babrius) in the second century A.D. Apart from the deduction from his linguistic style that he was a Hellenized Roman, nothing is known about the person Babrius. His collection included more than 200 fables, 143 of which are still extant in their original verse form, with an additional 57 having survived in prose paraphrases. Like the collection of his predecessor Phaedrus, Babrius's Aesopic fables also served as a source for later editors.

Among the many classical authors who used Aesop-like stories in their own works, none is more important than the Roman satirist and poet Horace (65–8 B.C.). In fact, one of the most famous of all fables attributed to Aesop, "The Town Mouse and the Country Mouse" (no. 141), was first recorded by Horace in his *Satires* (book 2, no. 6). The context is revealing, showing how traditional fables were used in classical Roman society. The narrator relates that from time to time a man named Cervius would tell fables to his friends, and whenever one of them would "forget the dreads of wealth, he'd tell this one." The narrator continues by recounting the now-familiar fable in full. Some 200 years later Babrius recorded "The Town Mouse and the Country Mouse" in his collection of Aesopic fables, and it has been credited to Aesop from that time forth.

### From the Middle Ages to the Present

Aesopic fables were highly valued in medieval and renaissance Europe for their ethical qualities, and many collections were assembled for educational use. The first of these were compilations in manuscript form and in Latin. An early and prominent example of these school texts was the compilation created in about 400 A.D. by Flavius Avianus, who rewrote in Latin verse 42 of the Greek fables from the Babrius collection. Although his stories lacked the compactness and the sharp focus of the best fables, his collection was nonetheless very influential in medieval Europe, and was often used in schools.

The development of movable-type printing, beginning about 1450, greatly facilitated the publication of fable collections in vernacular languages throughout Europe. In fact, apparently the first book printed in the German language was a collection of fables. (The famous Gutenberg Bible of 1455 was in Latin.) This collection was the work of Ulrich Boner, a Swiss Dominican monk, who in about 1350 compiled a manuscript collection of fables titled *Der Edelstein* (The Precious Stone) and attributed to Aesop and Flavius Avianus. After circulating for more than a century in manuscript form, *Der Edelstein* was printed as a book in 1461, and is reputed to be the first book printed in the German language.

Another German-language author, Heinrich Steinhöwel (1412–1483), contributed even more to the European distribution of Aesopic fables in the vernacular. His *Esopus*, a bilingual collection of fables in Latin and German, was published in about 1476 and soon became, relatively speaking, an international bestseller. This book was translated into French, Italian, Spanish, Dutch, and Czech. The French-language version of Steinhöwel's *Esopus* was translated into English and published in 1484 by William Caxton, the pioneering English printer. Thus a collection of Aesopic fables was also among the very first books published in the English language.

The popularity of fables attributed to Aesop from the Middle Ages onward led quite naturally to new literary creations in the same tradition. One such work was the so-called *Gesta Romanorum* (Deeds of the Romans), written in Latin by an anonymous English scribe about 1330. Only a few of the 283 recorded "deeds" relate to the Romans. Instead, the work presents a mixture of anecdotes, legends, and fables, all with appended morals, called "applications." About a dozen of the stories are animal fables, similar in content, form, and function to those of Aesop.

Medieval imitations of Aesop led to a new word in French, *ysopet* (also spelled *isopet*), referring to a collection of freshly minted fables in the Aesopic tradition. The most famous of these *ysopets* are the *Fables* of Marie de France, numbering 103 and composed in French verse between about 1160 and 1190. Although she is celebrated as the greatest woman author of the Middle Ages, almost nothing is known about the person Marie de France, except that she lived in French-speaking Norman England.

The re-creation of Aesopic fables in verse form was brought to its highest level some 500 years later by another French-language poet, Jean de La Fontaine (1621–1695). In about 240 poems, published in twelve books between 1668 and 1694, La Fontaine captured the essence of the Aesopic tradition with wit and charm. In fact, many readers of our era know Aesopic fables primarily through the graceful renditions of La Fontaine. The didactic nature of the fable, its pragmatic this-worldly view, and its roots in classical antiquity appealed to many other gifted European writers of the Age of Reason. Three additional names stand out: John Locke (1632–1704) and John Gay (1685–1732) from England, and Gotthold Ephraim Lessing (1729–1781) from Germany.

The nineteenth century produced two writers of beast stories deserving special notice. Possibly the greatest nineteenth-century author to rewrite Aesopic fables was Leo Tolstoy (1828–1910), who incorporated both traditional and original material into fables and fairy tales for primers and readers that he wrote in the 1870s to teach Russian peasants' children how to read. From a different world, but still drawing on the same traditional material, was Joel Chandler Harris (1848–1908), whose *Uncle Remus* stories contain many episodes also found in Aesopic fables. The prevailing view that African-American folklore provided much of Harris's raw material opens up the possibility that Africa may have played a substantial, but largely unheralded role in the development and transmission of Aesopic fables from the earliest times. Remember that according to some sources the man Aesop was a native of Ethiopia.

Many writers in the twentieth century have written imitations and parodies of traditional fables for their own social-critical purposes, but no one more successfully than the American humorist James Thurber (1894–1961) in his witty and ironic *Fables for Our Time* (1940). Also following in the satirical spirit of Aesop, if not imitating his terse style, was George Orwell (1903–1950), whose *Animal Farm* (1945) is often referred to as a "political fable."

The preceding list of editors and authors, covering more than 2,000 years of time and extending across the length and breadth of

Europe, and beyond, illustrates the timeless appeal of the Aesopic tradition. Many additional names could be added to the list. Aesopic fables are a cultural legacy whose importance can hardly be overstated.

## Oriental Fables

The history of Aesopic and Aesop-inspired fables in Europe outlined above follows a tradition beginning in Greece, nurtured in Rome, then expanded and brought to maturity throughout Europe, but this summary has not addressed the questions: Are similar didactic animal fables also native to cultures outside of Greece? And did such tales exist before Aesop? Both questions have affirmative answers, but supporting details are sketchy and sometimes ambiguous, as would be expected of evidence from the very distant past.

Clay tablets from ancient Mesopotamia have revealed the existence of collections of proverbs and fables featuring animals as actors some 4,000 years ago, and it is assumed that these tablets are based on even older material no longer extant. Did these Mesopotamian stories find their way to Greece and elsewhere in undisclosed prehistoric times, carried orally by ancient travelers? Or did the tales travel from Greece to Mesopotamia? These questions cannot be answered definitively, although experience with other forms of folklore and common sense itself suggest that some stories with universal application may well have been invented independently in more than one area, a process called polygenesis by folklorists. Furthermore, prehistoric travelers, like their modern counterparts, carried both material goods and intellectual property in all directions, both coming and going.

A large number of European folktales (especially the magic stories commonly called fairy tales) have their origin on the Indian subcontinent. Although the prevailing scholarly opinion of today is that Greece, not India, was the ancestral home of most animal fables, some of the latter country's most venerable literary works feature fables similar to those attributed to Aesop, and I find it hard to conceive that ancient Indian storytellers traveling abroad would omit animal fables from their repertory. In my judgment, the storytelling paths between ancient India and the Mediterranean world were two-way streets, to the mutual benefit of both cultures.

India's arguably most influential contribution to world literature is the *Panchatantra* (also spelled *Pañcatantra* or *Pañca-tantra*), which consists of five books of animal fables and magic tales (some 87 stories in all) that were compiled, in their current form, between the third and fifth centuries A.D. This work was based on an older Sanskrit collection, no longer extant, dating back as early as 100 B.C. It is believed that even then many of the stories were already ancient, having lived long lives as oral folktales. The anonymous compiler's self-proclaimed purpose was to educate his readers, a goal shared by publishers of Aesopic fables from the very beginning. Although the original author's or compiler's name is unknown, an Arabic translation from about 750 A.D. attributes the *Panchatantra* to a wise man called Bidpai. His name implies "court scholar" in Sanskrit, but nothing else is known about Bidpai as a person. Discussions of the fables in the *Panchatantra* inevitably lead to comparisons with Aesop, and indeed, about a dozen tales (or close variants) are found in both collections. Did the ancient Greeks learn these fables from Indian storytellers? Or was it the other way around? Again, a definitive answer probably will never be known, but given the rich narrative traditions of both cultures, it is unlikely that the influence was not mutual, with each side learning from and giving to the other.

Another great collection of didactic stories from India are the *Jataka* tales. Part of the canon of sacred Buddhist literature, this collection of some 550 anecdotes and fables depicts earlier births and incarnations—sometimes as an animal, sometimes as a human—of the being who would become Siddhartha Gautama, the future Buddha. Traditional birth and death dates of Gautama are 563–483 B.C. The *Jataka* tales are dated between 300 B.C. and 400 A.D., but many of them undoubtedly have antecedents in older folklore. A number of the *Jataka* fables have close parallels in Aesop.

Born and nurtured somewhat closer to Europe, and ultimately of even greater influence worldwide than the previously discussed two collections, is the great compilation of Arabic short fiction *The 1001 Nights*, also known as *The Arabian Nights' Entertainment*. Based on Indian, Persian, and Arabic folklore, this work dates back about 1,000 years as a unified collection, with many of its individual stories undoubtedly being even older. Although heralded primarily for its romantic tales of fantasy and magic, *The 1001 Nights* also contains a number of Aesop-like animal fables.

### The Fable as a Literary Genre

The fable, in keeping with its simple form, is easily defined. It is a short fictitious work, either in prose or in verse, frequently (but not necessarily) using animals or even inanimate objects as actors, and having the exposition of a moral principle as a primary function. It has an obvious relationship with other simple forms of literature such as the folk or fairy tale, the proverb, and the riddle. At their best, fables are compactly composed and, like all allegories, gain extended, unwritten meaning through the use of symbols.

Brevity is the fable's first requirement, with many of the best samples of the genre comprising only three or four sentences. "The Fox and the Grapes" (no. 1), with its mere three sentences, is exemplary in this regard. The first sentence sets the stage and introduces the problem: "A hungry fox saw some fine bunches of grapes hanging from a vine that was trained along a high trellis and did his best to reach them by jumping as high as he could into the air." The second sentence emphasizes the futility of the fox's efforts: "But it was all in vain, for they were just out of reach." And the final sentence describes how he salvaged psychological victory from physical defeat: "So he gave up trying and walked away with an air of dignity and unconcern, remarking, 'I thought those grapes were ripe, but I see now they are quite sour.'"

Viewed as an allegory—and to an extent all fables are simple allegories—the grapes represent any unattainable goal, and because from time to time all humans are confronted with impossibilities, the story assumes universal applicability. Interpreted symbolically, the story is thus more than the description of one individual seeking a single goal; it is the account of everyone pursuing fulfillment.

The crux of "The Fox and the Grapes" obviously is not the fox's failure to get the grapes, but rather his response to that failure. In essence, he rescues his dignity by lying to himself. However, the narrator makes no value judgment here, and precisely therein lies this fable's universal appeal. Each individual reader can respond to the fox's self-deception according to his or her own expectations and needs. We can criticize the fox for his dishonesty and inconsistency, or we can congratulate him for his pragmatism and positive self-image.

## The Moral of the Story

The essential quality of a fable is that it delivers a moral teaching, or, at the very least, that it presents an ethical problem, with or without a suggested solution. Modern readers have come to expect a fable to end with a succinct, proverb-like restatement of the moral illustrated by the tale. However, there is good reason to believe that in their original oral form, Aesopic fables stopped short of this restatement. After all, a well-crafted story does not require a summary any more than a well-told joke needs an explanation of the punch line. It could thus be argued that restating "the moral of the story" at the end of a fable is an insult both to the intelligence of the reader and to the skill of the author. Nevertheless, collectors and editors of Aesopic fables, almost from the beginning, have provided their readers with tacked-on explanations of some, if not most, of the fables in their collections.

In many of the oldest collections this statement comes at the beginning of the tale and describes its moral application. For example, in *The Aesopic Fables of Phaedrus* the familiar tale of "The Dog Carrying a Piece of Meat Across the River" is prefaced with the sentence "He who goes after what belongs to another deservedly loses his own" (Perry, p. 197). Such a preface, known to specialists as a *promythium* (plural, *promythia*), was probably not intended to be read or recited with the fable itself, but provided the readers with a suggestion as to how they might best use the fable to illustrate a point in a speech or literary composition. Furthermore, these succinct summaries served as guide words in published collections, helping the reader to find a fable illustrating a particular point of view.

Attached to the end of a fable, the moral application is called an *epimythium* (plural, *epimythia*), and this is the position favored by most editors during the nineteenth and twentieth centuries. In some instances the epimythium is not appended to the completed story, but constitutes a final statement by one of the characters. I offer but two from dozens of possible examples of this technique: "The Old Hound" (no. 126) ends with the old dog's complaint, "You ought to honor me for what I have been instead of abusing me for what I am." And "The Miller, His Son, and Their Ass" (no. 172) ends with the narrator's conclusion that the unfortunate miller was now convinced "that in trying to please all, he had pleased none."

### *Moral Philosophy*

What is the moral philosophy preached by the ancient Greek creators of Aesopic fables? "The Man and the Lion" (no. 80) concludes that "There are two sides to every question," a view that could serve not only as a moral for this one story, but also as a motto for almost the entire body of Aesopic fables. Given the prevailing view that these tales were actually composed and assembled by many different storytellers and editors, it should come as no surprise that the fables, in spite of their nearly unanimous interest in moral issues, do not form a self-consistent ethical system. In fact, quite the contrary is the case. Paradox, ambiguity, and irony permeate the collection.

Folklore wisdom often contradicts itself from one expression to another. "Absence makes the heart grow fonder" is a familiar and ostensibly time-proven proverb, but then so is its opposite, "Out of sight, out of mind." Some proverbs promote caution ("Look before you leap"), while others preach aggressiveness ("Nothing ventured, nothing gained"). "He who is not with me is against me" and "He who is not against me is with me" are equally familiar proverbial formulations with a biblical background.

Similarly, numerous pairs of Aesopic fables can be found that seemingly contradict each other. Are the contradictions unintentional oversights? Or do they represent the cynical view that there are no universal rules for ethical behavior? Here each individual reader must reach his or her own conclusion, and once again, that is part of the universal appeal of these fables.

My first example deals with the problem of vengeance. In "The Horse and the Stag" (no. 264) a horse recklessly avenges himself against a stag, but in the process loses his freedom. However, vengeful or hasty behavior does not always lead to injury. In "The Lion, the Wolf, and the Fox" (no. 255) a quick-thinking fox successfully takes revenge against a spiteful wolf by telling a sick lion that he can be cured by wrapping himself in the skin of a freshly killed wolf. Thus the morality proposed by these two stories, taken as a pair, is neither always to forgive one's enemies, nor to be consistently harsh in retribution, but rather, if the opportunity presents itself, to be cunningly clever in planning revenge.

The traditional virtue of loyalty presents another pair of examples. In "The Birds, the Beasts, and the Bat" (no. 168) a bat sides first with the birds, then with the beasts, and in the end is rejected by both groups as a double-faced traitor. On the other hand, in the fable "The Bat and the Weasels" (no. 7) a bat escapes from a weasel two times, first by claiming to be a mouse and later by claiming to be a bird.

The time-honored virtue of honesty provides yet another pair of contradictory fables. In "The Wolf and the Boy" (no. 171) a wolf captures a boy, but then spares his life as a reward for the boy having told the truth. "The Apes and the Two Travelers" (no. 44) reflects the opposite view. Here two strangers in the land of the apes are asked what they think of the king and his subjects. One of them lies, and is given a handsome reward; the other tells the truth (they are "fine apes"), and he is clawed to death for his honesty.

The view that "might makes right" is reflected in many animal fables, arguably offering license to the powerful to follow their own self-interests and urging the weak to remain submissive. Examples include "The Lion and the Wild Ass" (no. 107), "The Lion, the Fox, and the Ass" (no. 246), "The Wolf and the Lamb" (no. 11), and "The Cat and the Cock" (no. 116). But the opposite view is also represented. In one of the best-known of all Aesopic fables, "The Hare and the Tortoise" (no. 117), it is not the speedy hare who wins the race, but instead the contestant who, by racing standards, is seriously handicapped. Likewise, in the lesser-known fable "The Mouse and the Bull" (no. 139) a battle between very unevenly matched opponents does not go to the stronger of the two.

### Be True to Yourself

The previous section emphasizes fables, taken in pairs or small groups, that illustrate the unreliability, or at best the relativity of traditional moral rules. However, there are few, if any contradictions within the Aesopic collection to the Socratic admonition to know oneself and to be true to oneself. And in the Aesopic tradition knowing oneself also implies a resigned acceptance of that which cannot be changed about one's being and one's fate. Dozens of fables preach these views.

My first examples describe individuals who vainly try to assume the attributes of another (and presumably superior) group, only to be exposed, subjected to ridicule, or even put to death. In "The Ass and the Lapdog" (no. 32) an ass is severely beaten when he tries to imitate a pet dog by jumping into his master's lap. The fable ends with the ass's recognition of his own foolish behavior. In his own words, "Why could I not be satisfied with my natural and honorable position, without wishing to imitate the ridiculous antics of that useless little lapdog?" Similarly, in "The Monkey and the Camel" (no. 164) a camel tried to dance like a monkey, "but he cut such a ridiculous figure as he plunged about, and made such a grotesque exhibition of his ungainly person, that the beasts all fell upon him with ridicule and drove him away."

Numerous fables deride individuals who attempt to change their appearance by dressing in the clothes (or skin) of another. Such charades fail almost from the beginning. "The Ass in the Lion's Skin" (no. 61), "The Jackdaw and the Pigeons" (no. 70), and "The Vain Jackdaw" (no. 84) all conclude with the disguised individuals quickly being exposed and ridiculed. A character's altered appearance does not need to represent a desired change of identity. In "The Mice and the Weasels" (no. 96) the mice soldiers who before battle decorate themselves with large plumes are easily captured and killed by their opponents.

Fables about trying to change one's appearance often have racial (even racist) overtones. In two stories, "The Crow and the Swan" (no. 148) and "The Blackamoor" (no. 105), attempts are made to wash black individuals white, with predictably unhappy results. These particular stories take on a special poignancy when one recalls that Aesop himself was said to have had very dark-colored skin.

Failure to know and to accept oneself as one is does not always manifest itself in altered appearance. Often it is vain, pretentious behavior alone that exposes the character to ridicule. In "The Eagle, the Jackdaw, and the Shepherd" (no. 170) a jackdaw tries to perform like an eagle. In "The Crow and the Raven" (no. 259) a crow imitates a raven. In "The Ox and the Frog" (no. 100) a mother frog tries to puff herself up to the size of an ox. In "The Wolf and His Shadow" (no. 238) a wolf sees his long shadow when the sun is low in the sky, perceives himself to be very large, then struts about in a manner befitting a giant. And in "The Tortoise and the Eagle" (no. 81) a tortoise tries to learn to fly. All these attempts end with ridicule or death for the pretenders.

Aesopic fables reflect a society structured by class and privilege, and although the stories seem to have come from the lower classes (remember that both Aesop and Phaedrus were reputed to have been born as slaves), they do little to encourage an individual to rise above his or her original station in life. To the contrary, a number of fables illustrate the moral "Better servitude with safety than freedom with danger"—for example, "The Fox Who Served a Lion" (no. 253) and "The Pack Ass, the Wild Ass, and the Lion" (no. 201). Similarly, in "The Ass and His Masters" (no. 200) a beast of burden, over-worked and abused by his owner, prays for a new master, only to find himself in a worse situation, then prays again for another new master, and his situation worsens again. Finally, in "The Runaway Slave" (no. 270) the fugitive is soon recaptured, and we are given to believe that he too will henceforth be much worse off than before his attempted escape.

### *Practical Everyday Advice*

In keeping with their folklore heritage, Aesopic fables reflect the lifestyle, the values, and the frustrations of ordinary people in classical antiquity: slaves, peasants, workers, and tradespeople. These stories are not liberal treatises about self-determination and upward mobility. To the contrary, they more often preach a philosophy of acceptance and resignation. However, they do offer consoling, pragmatic advice that can make life easier even for the disenfranchised and the poor.

"Do not grieve too long at the death of a loved one" is the message of "Grief and His Due" (no. 276). "A bird in the hand is worth two in the bush" is the proverbial sentiment embodied in a number of fables, including "The Dog and His Reflection" (no. 94) and "The Lion and the Hare" (no. 183). "Do not trust the words of your enemies" is the lesson that emerges from "The Wolf, the Mother, and Her Child" (no. 112). "Father and Sons" (no. 58) and "The Lion and the Three Bulls" (no. 122) emphasize the value of unity. "The Grasshopper and the Ants" (no. 156) shows the utility of thrift and industry. "The Shepherd's Boy and the Wolf" (no. 46) admonishes honesty, not so much as an absolute ethical standard, but more as a pragmatic practice, because, as the moral of the story states, "You cannot believe a liar even when he tells the truth." "The Goose That Laid the Golden Eggs" (no. 2) preaches against greed, but again, not as an abstract principle, but rather as a practical way to avoid catastrophic loss.

"The Oak and the Reeds" (no. 41) perhaps provides the capstone to the pragmatic moral philosophy of Aesop. An oak tree, sturdy and unwavering, is uprooted by a severe storm, whereas some reeds, bowing and yielding to every breeze, survive without injury. The moral of this story is too obvious to require restatement.

### Reflection of Human Psychology

Many of the best-known Aesopic fables refrain from overt preaching, depicting instead selected episodes of human behavior, without comment. Aesop thus holds a mirror up to humanity, and he does not always like the reflection that he sees. However, he does not need to burden his depictions with explicit value judgments. The perceptive reader will understand.

"The Sick Stag" (no. 177) is the timeless tale of a sick animal surrounded by well-wishers who thoughtlessly eat all the nearby grass, thus inadvertently causing their friend to perish from hunger. The central character in "The Miser" (no. 262) gloats over his treasure but makes no practical use of it. The fox without a tail, in the fable bearing that title (no. 83), having lost his own tail in a trap, tries to talk all his fellow foxes into cutting off their tails to divert attention from his own loss. Another fox, in "The Foxes and the River" (no. 263), recklessly steps into a river and is swept away, but he refuses to admit that he has made a mistake and pretends to be going for a leisurely swim. Open a collection of Aesop's fables at random, and you will almost certainly find a tale reflecting an unpleasant aspect of human behavior and psychology.

## Etiological Tales

An important function of folklore and mythology in all cultures is to offer explanations as to why things are as they are. Specialists refer to such explanatory tales as etiological tales, stories about causes. They are also called *pourquoi* tales from the French word for "why." These accounts can be religiously serious or playfully fictitious. There are many etiological tales among the fables of Aesop, and they belong almost exclusively to the playful category. The previously quoted admonition of Phaedrus, the compiler of the oldest Aesop collection still extant, is of special significance with reference to etiological tales: "Remember that I speak in jest of things that never happened."

Etiological tales by a different author and in another context can take on the gravity of a creation myth, but it is unlikely that the ancient Greeks took very seriously the humorous Aesopic account as to why the tortoise carries his house on his back as recorded in "Jupiter and the Tortoise" (no. 71). Similarly, "Mercury and the Tradesmen" (no. 95), an explanation as to why all tradesmen lie, but especially the horse dealers, is much more of a "used-car salesman joke" than it is a theological treatise, in spite of its reference to one of the classical deities. Yet another lighthearted Aesopic etiological fable invoking a deity is "The Bee and Jupiter" (no. 40), which explains why bees have barbed stingers that cost them their lives when they use them.

Even those etiological fables that comment on grave philosophical issues do so in a playful manner. I let three examples suffice: "The Man, the Horse, the Ox, and the Dog" (no. 234) justifies the increasingly difficult stages of human life as one ages. "The Goods and the Ills" (no. 24) shows why there appears to be more evil than good on earth. And "Prometheus and the Making of Man" (no. 279) explains why some people have the bodies of men but the souls of beasts. These are weighty topics, and the brief fables that address them do not claim to solve the problems that they embody, but then neither do they simply brush such problems aside, pretending that they do not exist.

## Religion

Moral involvement is a quintessential function of the fable, which will often translate into discussions of religion, given the close association in most, if not all cultures between morality and religion. It should thus come as no surprise that religion plays a central role in many of the Aesopic fables.

The religion in question is, of course, that of the ancient Greeks, as interpreted by the Romans, through whose intermediacy the fables have come to us. Thus most of the deities mentioned are identified by their Roman instead of their Greek names. (At the end of this book is a glossary describing the classical gods and heroes featured in the present collection of Aesopic fables.)

The Greeks and Romans did not worship a single, all-powerful, all-benevolent god, but instead recognized an assemblage of deities with varying degrees of power and sometimes bewildering and seemingly contradictory aims and expectations. The resulting ambivalence in the relationship between mortals and the deities surfaces repeatedly in Aesopic fables, some of which depict the great power of the gods, whereas others emphasize their apparent impotence.

Typical of fables reflecting the deities' weakness is "The Man Who Lost His Spade" (no. 268), in which a farmer goes to a temple in the city, hoping there to gain information from the gods about a stolen spade. Upon his arrival he learns that a reward is being offered for the return of goods stolen from the temple. He concludes, "If these town gods can't detect the thieves who steal from their own temples, it's scarcely likely they can tell me who stole my spade." Even more cynical is "The Man and the Image" (no. 101), in which a man destroys a sacred idol for its unwillingness or inability to grant him riches, and then is rewarded as a direct consequence of his sacrilegious act. Additional fables depicting the weakness of the gods and their prophets include "Mercury and the Sculptor" (no. 88), "The Image Seller" (no. 109), "The Prophet" (no. 130), and "The Eagle and the Beetle" (no. 223).

In other fables the opposite claim is made, namely that omnis-

cient gods will indeed reward moral behavior and punish evil. For
example, in "The Butcher and His Customers" (no. 251) a butcher,
having lost a piece of meat to two lying thieves, concludes, "You
may cheat me with your lying, but you can't cheat the gods, and
they won't let you off so lightly." Nor do the gods necessarily wait
until the next life to reward virtue and punish vice, as evidenced in
the fable "Mercury and the Woodman" (no. 17), in which a god
rewards an honest woodcutter with a golden ax and a silver ax, in
addition to the ordinary one that he had lost in a river, while a
dishonest companion loses everything. Other examples of omnis-
cient divine intervention are found in "The Rogue and the Oracle"
(no. 273), where the Oracle at Delphi exposes a scoundrel who
attempts to ridicule a venerable religious institution, and in "The
Eagle and the Fox" (no. 250), with its conclusion that "False faith
may escape human punishment, but cannot escape the divine."

The examples from the previous paragraph notwithstanding, the
moral view reflected in most of the Aesopic fables is human-
centered and of this world. In "The Astronomer" (no. 187) the leading character is so absorbed by his vision of the sky that he falls into
a dry well. Adding insult to injury, a cynical passerby chides him,
"If you . . . were looking so hard at the sky that you didn't even see
where your feet were carrying you along the ground, it appears to
me that you deserve all you've got." Mortals themselves, not the
gods, bear the primary responsibility for their own welfare. Only
rarely do the deities of these fables intervene on man's behalf. Even
if they were able to, which is no sure thing, the gods could not
possibly answer all of humankind's prayers, for they often contradict
one another, as stated explicitly in "The Father and His Daughters"
(no. 197), when a father, desiring to pray for his two daughters'
happiness, learns that one of them, a gardener's wife, wants rain,
while the other one, a potter's wife, wants dry weather. In the end,
as we learn either implicitly or explicitly from "The Snake and Jupiter" (no. 237) and "Hercules and the Wagoner" (no. 102), the
gods help those who help themselves.

### Fables and Folklore

"I already know this story" is a common response, even to first-time
readers of Aesop. And for good reason, for many of these fables

have found their way back into the repertories of oral storytellers, thus creating for themselves a new life independent of paper and ink. Most of these tales probably came from the folk in the first place, having long circulated as retold stories before they were committed to parchment or paper. The first creation of these fables lies too far in the past for us to be able to ascertain whether a particular tale was originated by a Greek scholar, quill pen in hand, or by an illiterate grandmother entertaining her extended family with bedtime stories. Whatever their origin, many of Aesop's fables have had a life of their own as orally told folktales, some having escaped the boundaries of the printed page at a relatively late date, others having followed unwritten folkways from the very beginning.

Folklorists use a cataloging system devised by the Finnish scholar Antti Aarne and his American counterpart Stith Thompson. The final version of this system was published in 1961 under the title *The Types of the Folktale*, and has proven itself an indispensable tool for the comparative study of international folktales. In essence, Aarne and Thompson identify some 2,500 basic folktale plots, assigning to each a type number, sometimes further differentiated by letters or asterisks. Only those Aesopic fables that have been found in folklore sources apart from Aesop have been assigned Aarne-Thompson type numbers. These fables, characteristically and understandably among the best known, are identified by their type numbers in an appendix to the present collection.

### Modern Translations of Aesop

Editors and translators of every age must come to terms with essentially the same questions: What text shall I use for my source? And what style shall I adopt for the finished product? As already noted, the absence of any canon or standard edition of Aesop's fables has made the first question particularly problematic. Most modern editors use a combination of fables found in the classical editions of Phaedrus and Babrius, supplemented by various medieval and renaissance collections. As to style, well into the twentieth century most English translators of Aesop have seemed to prefer intentionally antiquated language, sprinkling their texts with archaic words and outdated grammar. Fortunately, V. S. Vernon Jones, the translator of the present collection, resisted this temptation. His English is sprightly, concise, and idiomatic, just as the everyday Greek used by the original storytellers must have been. Jones's translation was published under the title *Æsop's Fables* in 1912 by W. Heinemann of London. I have added footnotes, cautiously modernized the punctuation, and brought the spelling to contemporary American standards, but have made essentially no other revisions to his admirable text.

---

**D. L. Ashliman** received a B.A. degree from the University of Utah, and M.A. and Ph.D. degrees from Rutgers University, with additional studies at the Universities of Bonn and Göttingen in Germany. He taught folklore, mythology, German, and comparative literature at the University of Pittsburgh for thirty-three years and was emeritized in the year 2000. In addition to teaching, he held a number of administrative positions at the University of Pittsburgh, including Academic Dean for the Semester at Sea program. He also served as a guest professor in the departments of comparative literature and folklore at the University of Augsburg in Germany. D. L. Ashliman is the author of *A Guide to Folktales in the English Language*, published by Greenwood Press in 1987, as well as numerous articles and conference reports.

# AESOP'S FABLES

# CONTENTS

## 1 . THE FOX AND THE GRAPES

A hungry fox saw some fine bunches of grapes hanging from a vine that was trained along a high trellis and did his best to reach them by jumping as high as he could into the air. But it was all in vain, for they were just out of reach. So he gave up trying and walked away with an air of dignity and unconcern, remarking, "I thought those grapes were ripe, but I see now they are quite sour."

## 2 . THE GOOSE THAT LAID THE GOLDEN EGGS

A man and his wife had the good fortune to possess a goose which laid a golden egg every day. Lucky though they were, they soon began to think they were not getting rich fast enough, and, imagining the bird must be made of gold inside, they decided to kill it in order to secure the whole store of precious metal at once. But when they cut it open they found it was just like any other goose. Thus, they neither got rich all at once, as they had hoped, nor enjoyed any longer the daily addition to their wealth.

**Much wants more and loses all.**

## 3 · THE CAT AND THE MICE

There was once a house that was overrun with mice. A cat heard of this and said to herself, "That's the place for me." And off she went and took up her quarters in the house and caught the mice one by one and ate them. At last the mice could stand it no longer, and they determined to take to their holes and stay there. "That's awkward," said the cat to herself. "The only thing to do is to coax them out by a trick." So she considered awhile, and then climbed up the wall and let herself hang down by her hind legs from a peg and pretended to be dead. By and by a mouse peeped out and saw the cat hanging there. "Aha!" it cried. "You're very clever, madam, no doubt; but you may turn yourself into a bag of meal hanging there, if you like, yet you won't catch us coming anywhere near you."

**If you are wise you won't be deceived by the innocent airs of those whom you have once found to be dangerous.**

## 4 · THE MISCHIEVOUS DOG

There was once a dog who used to snap at people and bite them without any provocation, and who was a great nuisance to everyone who came to his master's house. So his master fastened a bell round his neck to warn people of his presence. The dog was very proud of the bell, and strutted about tinkling it with immense satisfaction. But an old dog came up to him and said, "The fewer airs you give yourself the better, my friend. You don't think, do you, that your bell was given you as a reward of merit? On the contrary, it is a badge of disgrace."

**Notoriety is often mistaken for fame.**

## 5 · THE CHARCOAL BURNER AND THE FULLER

There was once a charcoal burner who lived and worked by himself. A fuller,* however, happened to come and settle in the same neighborhood; and the charcoal burner, having made his acquaintance and finding he was an agreeable sort of fellow, asked him if he would come and share his house. "We shall get to know one another better that way," he said, "and, besides, our household expenses will be diminished." The fuller thanked him, but replied, "I couldn't think of it, sir. Why, everything I take such pains to whiten would be blackened in no time by your charcoal."

---

*A fuller bleached and thickened woolen cloth through a boiling and pounding process.

# 6. THE MICE IN COUNCIL

Once upon a time all the mice met together in council and discussed the best means of securing themselves against the attacks of the cat. After several suggestions had been debated, a mouse of some standing and experience got up and said, "I think I have hit upon a plan which will ensure our safety in the future, provided you approve and carry it out. It is that we should fasten a bell round the neck of our enemy the cat, which will by its tinkling warn us of her approach." This proposal was warmly applauded, and it had been already decided to adopt it, when an old mouse got upon his feet and said, "I agree with you all that the plan before us is an admirable one. But may I ask who is going to bell the cat?"

## 7 · THE BAT AND THE WEASELS

A bat fell to the ground and was caught by a weasel, and was just going to be killed and eaten when it begged to be let go. The weasel said he couldn't do that because he was an enemy of all birds on principle. "Oh, but," said the bat, "I'm not a bird at all. I'm a mouse." "So you are," said the weasel, "now I come to look at you." And he let it go. Some time after this the bat was caught in just the same way by another weasel, and, as before, begged for its life. "No," said the weasel, "I never let a mouse go by any chance." "But I'm not a mouse," said the bat. "I'm a bird." "Why, so you are," said the weasel. And he too let the bat go.

**Look and see which way the wind blows before you commit yourself.**

## 8 · THE DOG AND THE SOW

A dog and a sow were arguing, and each claimed that its own young ones were finer than those of any other animal. "Well," said the sow at last, "mine can see, at any rate, when they come into the world; but yours are born blind."

THE FOX AND THE CROW

## 9 . THE FOX AND THE CROW

A crow was sitting on a branch of a tree with a piece of cheese in her beak when a fox observed her and set his wits to work to discover some way of getting the cheese. Coming and standing under the tree he looked up and said, "What a noble bird I see above me! Her beauty is without equal, the hue of her plumage exquisite. If only her voice is as sweet as her looks are fair, she ought without doubt to be queen of the birds." The crow was hugely flattered by this, and just to show the fox that she could sing she gave a loud caw. Down came the cheese, of course, and the fox, snatching it up, said, "You have a voice, madam, I see. What you want is wits."

## 10.   THE HORSE AND THE GROOM

There was once a groom who used to spend long hours clipping and combing the horse of which he had charge, but who daily stole a portion of its allowance of oats, and sold it for his own profit. The horse gradually got into worse and worse condition, and at last cried to the groom, "If you really want me to look sleek and well, you must comb me less and feed me more."

## 11. THE WOLF AND THE LAMB

A wolf came upon a lamb straying from the flock, and felt some compunction about taking the life of so helpless a creature without some plausible excuse. So he cast about for a grievance and said at last, "Last year, sirrah, you grossly insulted me." "That is impossible, sir," bleated the lamb, "for I wasn't born then." "Well," retorted the wolf, "you feed in my pastures." "That cannot be," replied the lamb, "for I have never yet tasted grass." "You drink from my spring, then," continued the wolf. "Indeed, sir," said the poor lamb, "I have never yet drunk anything but my mother's milk." "Well, anyhow," said the wolf, "I'm not going without my dinner." And he sprang upon the lamb and devoured it without more ado.

## 12. THE PEACOCK AND THE CRANE

A peacock taunted a crane with the dullness of her plumage. "Look at my brilliant colors," said she, "and see how much finer they are than your poor feathers." "I am not denying," replied the crane, "that yours are far gayer than mine. But when it comes to flying I can soar into the clouds, whereas you are confined to the earth like any dunghill cock."

THE CAT AND THE BIRDS

## 13. THE CAT AND THE BIRDS

A cat heard that the birds in an aviary were ailing. So he got himself up as a doctor, and, taking with him a set of the instruments proper to his profession, presented himself at the door, and inquired after the health of the birds. "We shall do very well," they replied, without letting him in, "when we've seen the last of you."

A villain may disguise himself, but he will not deceive the wise.

## 14. THE SPENDTHRIFT AND
## THE SWALLOW

A spendthrift, who had wasted his fortune and had nothing left but the clothes in which he stood, saw a swallow one fine day in early spring. Thinking that summer had come and that he could now do without his coat, he went and sold it for what it would fetch. A change, however, took place in the weather, and there came a sharp frost which killed the unfortunate swallow. When the spendthrift saw its dead body he cried, "Miserable bird! Thanks to you I am perishing of cold myself."

**One swallow does not make summer.**

## 15. THE OLD WOMAN AND
## THE DOCTOR

An old woman became almost totally blind from a disease of the eyes, and, after consulting a doctor, made an agreement with him in the presence of witnesses that she should pay him a high fee if he cured her, while if he failed he was to receive nothing. The doctor accordingly prescribed a course of treatment, and every time he paid her a visit he took away with him some article out of the house, until at last, when he visited her for the last time, and the cure was complete, there was nothing left.

When the old woman saw that the house was empty she refused to pay him his fee; and, after repeated refusals on her part, he sued her before the magistrates for payment of her debt. On being brought into court she was ready with her defense. "The claimant," said she, "has stated the facts about our agreement correctly. I undertook to pay him a fee if he cured me, and he, on his part, promised to charge nothing if he failed. Now, he says I am cured. But I say that I am blinder than ever, and I can prove what I say. When my eyes were bad I could at any rate see well enough to be aware that my house contained a certain amount of furniture and other things. But now, when according to him I am cured, I am entirely unable to see anything there at all."

THE MOON AND HER MOTHER

## 16. THE MOON AND HER MOTHER

The moon once begged her mother to make her a gown. "How can I?" replied she. "There's no fitting your figure. At one time you're a new moon, and at another you're a full moon; and between whiles you're neither one nor the other."

## 17. MERCURY AND THE WOODMAN

A woodman was felling a tree on the bank of a river, when his ax, glancing off the trunk, flew out of his hands and fell into the water. As he stood by the water's edge lamenting his loss, Mercury appeared and asked him the reason for his grief; and on learning what had happened, out of pity for his distress he dived into the river and, bringing up a golden ax, asked him if that was the one he had lost. The woodman replied that it was not, and Mercury then dived a second time and, bringing up a silver ax, asked if that was his. "No, that is not mine either," said the woodman. Once more Mercury dived into the river, and brought up the missing ax. The woodman was overjoyed at recovering his property, and thanked his benefactor warmly; and the latter was so pleased with his honesty that he made him a present of the other two axes.

When the woodman told the story to his companions, one of these was filled with envy of his good fortune and determined to try his luck for himself. So he went and began to fell a tree at the edge of the river, and presently contrived to let his ax drop into the water.

Mercury appeared as before, and, on learning that his ax had fallen in, he dived and brought up a golden ax, as he had done on the previous occasion. Without waiting to be asked whether it was his or not the fellow cried, "That's mine, that's mine," and stretched out his hand eagerly for the prize. But Mercury was so disgusted at his dishonesty that he not only declined to give him the golden ax, but also refused to recover for him the one he had let fall into the stream.

**Honesty is the best policy.**

## 18. THE ASS, THE FOX, AND THE LION

An ass and a fox went into partnership and sallied out to forage for food together. They hadn't gone far before they saw a lion coming their way, at which they were both dreadfully frightened. But the fox thought he saw a way of saving his own skin, and went boldly up to the lion and whispered in his ear, "I'll manage that you shall get hold of the ass without the trouble of stalking him, if you'll promise to let me go free." The lion agreed to this, and the fox then rejoined his companion and contrived before long to lead him by a hidden pit, which some hunter had dug as a trap for wild animals, and into which he fell. When the lion saw that the ass was safely caught and couldn't get away, it was to the fox that he first turned his attention, and he soon finished him off, and then at his leisure proceeded to feast upon the ass.

**Betray a friend, and you'll often find you have ruined yourself.**

## 19. THE LION AND THE MOUSE

A lion asleep in his lair was waked up by a mouse running over his face. Losing his temper he seized it with his paw and was about to kill it. The mouse, terrified, piteously entreated him to spare its life. "Please let me go," it cried, "and one day I will repay you for your kindness." The idea of so insignificant a creature ever being able to do anything for him amused the lion so much that he laughed aloud, and good-humoredly let it go. But the mouse's chance came, after all. One day the lion got entangled in a net which had been spread for game by some hunters, and the mouse heard and recognized his roars of anger and ran to the spot. Without more ado it set to work to gnaw the ropes with its teeth, and succeeded before long in setting the lion free. "There!" said the mouse, "you laughed at me when I promised I would repay you. But now you see, even a mouse can help a lion."

## 20. THE CROW AND THE PITCHER

A thirsty crow found a pitcher with some water in it, but so little was there that, try as she might, she could not reach it with her beak, and it seemed as though she would die of thirst within sight of the remedy. At last she hit upon a clever plan. She began dropping pebbles into the pitcher, and with each pebble the water rose a little higher until at last it reached the brim, and the knowing bird was enabled to quench her thirst.

**Necessity is the mother of invention.**

## 21. THE BOYS AND THE FROGS

S ome mischievous boys were playing on the edge of a pond, and, catching sight of some frogs swimming about in the shallow water, they began to amuse themselves by pelting them with stones, and they killed several of them. At last one of the frogs put his head out of the water and said, "Oh, stop! Stop! I beg of you. What is sport to you is death to us."

**THE NORTH WIND AND THE SUN**

## 22. THE NORTH WIND AND THE SUN

A dispute arose between the north wind and the sun, each claiming that he was stronger than the other. At last they agreed to try their powers upon a traveler, to see which could soonest strip him of his cloak. The north wind had the first try; and, gathering up all his force for the attack, he came whirling furiously down upon the man, and caught up his cloak as though he would wrest it from him by one single effort. But the harder he blew, the more closely the man wrapped it round himself. Then came the turn of the sun. At first he beamed gently upon the traveler, who soon unclasped his cloak and walked on with it hanging loosely about his shoulders. Then he shone forth in his full strength, and the man, before he had gone many steps, was glad to throw his cloak right off and complete his journey more lightly clad.

**Persuasion is better than force.**

## 23. THE MISTRESS AND HER SERVANTS

A widow, thrifty and industrious, had two servants, whom she kept pretty hard at work. They were not allowed to lie long abed in the mornings, but the old lady had them up and doing as soon as the cock crew. They disliked intensely having to get up at such an hour, especially in wintertime; and they thought that if it were not for the cock waking up their mistress so horribly early, they could sleep longer. So they caught it and wrung its neck. But they weren't prepared for the consequences. For what happened was that their mistress, not hearing the cock crow as usual, waked them up earlier than ever, and set them to work in the middle of the night.

## 24. THE GOODS AND THE ILLS

There was a time in the youth of the world when goods and ills entered equally into the concerns of men, so that the goods did not prevail to make them altogether blessed, nor the ills to make them wholly miserable. But owing to the foolishness of mankind the ills multiplied greatly in number and increased in strength, until it seemed as though they would deprive the goods of all share in human affairs, and banish them from the earth.

The latter, therefore, betook themselves to heaven and complained to Jupiter of the treatment they had received, at the same time praying him to grant them protection from the ills, and to advise them concerning the manner of their intercourse with men. Jupiter granted their request for protection, and decreed that for the future they should not go among men openly in a body, and so be liable to attack from the hostile ills, but singly and unobserved, and at infrequent and unexpected intervals. Hence it is that the earth is full of ills, for they come and go as they please and are never far away; while goods, alas, come one by one only, and have to travel all the way from heaven, so that they are very seldom seen.

## 25. THE HARES AND THE FROGS

The hares once gathered together and lamented the unhappiness of their lot, exposed as they were to dangers on all sides and lacking the strength and the courage to hold their own. Men, dogs, birds, and beasts of prey were all their enemies, and killed and devoured them daily; and sooner than endure such persecution any longer, they one and all determined to end their miserable lives. Thus resolved and desperate, they rushed in a body towards a neighboring pool, intending to drown themselves. On the bank were sitting a number of frogs, who, when they heard the noise of the hares as they ran, with one accord leaped into the water and hid themselves in the depths. Then one of the older hares who was wiser than the rest cried out to his companions, "Stop, my friends, take heart. Don't let us destroy ourselves after all. See, here are creatures who are afraid of us, and who must, therefore, be still more timid than ourselves."

## 2 6 .   T H E   F O X   A N D   T H E   S T O R K

A fox invited a stork to dinner, at which the only fare provided was a large flat dish of soup. The fox lapped it up with great relish, but the stork with her long bill tried in vain to partake of the savory broth. Her evident distress caused the sly fox much amusement. But not long after, the stork invited him in turn, and set before him a pitcher with a long and narrow neck, into which she could get her bill with ease. Thus, while she enjoyed her dinner, the fox sat by hungry and helpless, for it was impossible for him to reach the tempting contents of the vessel.

## 27. THE WOLF IN SHEEP'S CLOTHING

A wolf resolved to disguise himself in order that he might prey upon a flock of sheep without fear of detection. So he clothed himself in a sheepskin and slipped among the sheep when they were out at pasture. He completely deceived the shepherd, and when the flock was penned for the night he was shut in with the rest. But that very night, as it happened, the shepherd, requiring a supply of mutton for the table, laid hands on the wolf in mistake for a sheep, and killed him with his knife on the spot.

## 28. THE STAG IN THE OX STALL

A stag, chased from his lair by the hounds, took refuge in a farmyard, and, entering a stable where a number of oxen were stalled, thrust himself under a pile of hay in a vacant stall, where he lay concealed, all but the tips of his horns. Presently one of the oxen said to him, "What has induced you to come in here? Aren't you aware of the risk you are running of being captured by the herdsmen?" To which he replied, "Pray let me stay for the present. When night comes I shall easily escape under cover of the dark." In the course of the afternoon more than one of the farm-hands came in to attend to the wants of the cattle, but not one of them noticed the presence of the stag, who accordingly began to congratulate himself on his escape and to express his gratitude to the oxen.

"We wish you well," said the one who had spoken before, "but you are not out of danger yet. If the master comes you will certainly be found out, for nothing ever escapes his keen eyes." Presently, sure enough, in he came, and made a great to-do about the way the oxen were kept. "The beasts are starving," he cried. "Here, give them more hay, and put plenty of litter under them." As he spoke, he seized an armful himself from the pile where the stag lay concealed, and at once detected him. Calling his men, he had him seized at once and killed for the table.

## 29. THE MILKMAID AND HER PAIL

A farmer's daughter had been out to milk the cows and was returning to the dairy carrying her pail of milk upon her head. As she walked along, she fell a-musing after this fashion: "The milk in this pail will provide me with cream, which I will make into butter and take to market to sell. With the money I will buy a number of eggs, and these, when hatched, will produce chickens, and by and by I shall have quite a large poultry yard. Then I shall sell some of my fowls, and with the money which they will bring in I will buy myself a new gown, which I shall wear when I go to the fair. And all the young fellows will admire it, and come and make love to me, but I shall toss my head and have nothing to say to them." Forgetting all about the pail, and suiting the action to the word, she tossed her head. Down went the pail, all the milk was spilled, and all her fine castles in the air vanished in a moment!

**Do not count your chickens before they are hatched.**

## 30. THE DOLPHINS, THE WHALES, AND THE SPRAT

The dolphins quarreled with the whales, and before very long they began fighting with one another. The battle was very fierce, and had lasted some time without any sign of coming to an end, when a sprat thought that perhaps he could stop it; so he stepped in and tried to persuade them to give up fighting and make friends. But one of the dolphins said to him contemptuously, "We would rather go on fighting till we're all killed than be reconciled by a sprat like you!"

## 31. THE FOX AND THE MONKEY

A fox and a monkey were on the road together and fell into a dispute as to which of the two was the better born. They kept it up for some time, till they came to a place where the road passed through a cemetery full of monuments, when the monkey stopped and looked about him and gave a great sigh. "Why do you sigh?" said the fox. The monkey pointed to the tombs and replied, "All the monuments that you see here were put up in honor of my forefathers, who in their day were eminent men." The fox was speechless for a moment, but quickly recovering he said, "Oh! Don't stop at any lie, sir; you're quite safe. I'm sure none of your ancestors will rise up and expose you."

**Boasters brag most when they cannot be detected.**

## 32. THE ASS AND THE LAPDOG

There was once a man who had an ass and a lapdog. The ass was housed in the stable with plenty of oats and hay to eat and was as well off as an ass could be. The little dog was made a great pet of by his master, who fondled him and often let him lie in his lap. And if he went out to dinner, he would bring back a tidbit or two to give him when he ran to meet him on his return. The ass had, it is true, a good deal of work to do, carting or grinding the corn,* or carrying the burdens of the farm; and ere long he became very jealous, contrasting his own life of labor with the ease and idleness of the lapdog. At last one day he broke his halter, and frisking into the house just as his master sat down to dinner, he pranced and capered about, mimicking the frolics of the little favorite, upsetting the table and smashing the crockery with his clumsy efforts. Not content with that, he even tried to jump on his master's lap, as he had so often seen the dog allowed to do. At that the servants, seeing the danger their master was in, belabored the silly ass with sticks and cudgels, and drove him back to his stable half dead with his beating. "Alas!" he cried. "All this I have brought on myself. Why could I not be satisfied with my natural and honorable position, without wishing to imitate the ridiculous antics of that useless little lapdog?"

---

*The word "corn" designates any type of grain.

THE FIR TREE AND THE BRAMBLE

## 33. THE FIR TREE AND THE BRAMBLE

A fir tree was boasting to a bramble, and said, somewhat contemptuously, "You poor creature, you are of no use whatever. Now, look at me. I am useful for all sorts of things, particularly when men build houses; they can't do without me then." But the bramble replied, "Ah, that's all very well, but you wait till they come with axes and saws to cut you down, and then you'll wish you were a bramble and not a fir."

**Better poverty without a care than wealth with its many obligations.**

## 34. THE FROGS' COMPLAINT AGAINST THE SUN

Once upon a time the sun was about to take to himself a wife. The frogs in terror all raised their voices to the skies, and Jupiter, disturbed by the noise, asked them what they were croaking about. They replied, "The sun is bad enough even while he is single, drying up our marshes with his heat as he does. But what will become of us if he marries and begets other suns?"

## 35 · THE DOG, THE COCK,
## AND THE FOX

A dog and a cock became great friends and agreed to travel together. At nightfall the cock flew up into the branches of a tree to roost, while the dog curled himself up inside the trunk, which was hollow. At break of day the cock woke up and crew, as usual. A fox heard, and, wishing to make a breakfast of him, came and stood under the tree and begged him to come down. "I should so like," said he, "to make the acquaintance of one who has such a beautiful voice." The cock replied, "Would you just wake my porter who sleeps at the foot of the tree? He'll open the door and let you in." The fox accordingly rapped on the trunk, when out rushed the dog and tore him in pieces.

## 36. THE GNAT AND THE BULL

A gnat alighted on one of the horns of a bull, and remained sitting there for a considerable time. When it had rested sufficiently and was about to fly away, it said to the bull, "Do you mind if I go now?" The bull merely raised his eyes and remarked, without interest, "It's all one to me. I didn't notice when you came, and I shan't know when you go away."

We may often be of more consequence in our own eyes than in the eyes of our neighbors.

## 37 · THE BEAR AND THE TRAVELERS

Two travelers were on the road together when a bear suddenly appeared on the scene. Before he observed them, one made for a tree at the side of the road and climbed up into the branches and hid there. The other was not so nimble as his companion; and, as he could not escape, he threw himself on the ground and pretended to be dead. The bear came up and sniffed all round him, but he kept perfectly still and held his breath, for they say that a bear will not touch a dead body. The bear took him for a corpse and went away. When the coast was clear, the traveler in the tree came down and asked the other what it was the bear had whispered to him when he put his mouth to his ear. The other replied, "He told me never again to travel with a friend who deserts you at the first sign of danger."

**Misfortune tests the sincerity of friendship.**

## 38 · THE SLAVE AND THE LION

A slave* ran away from his master, by whom he had been most cruelly treated, and, in order to avoid capture, betook himself into the desert. As he wandered about in search of food and shelter, he came to a cave, which he entered and found to be

---

*In some versions the slave is known by the name Androcles.

unoccupied. Really, however, it was a lion's den, and almost immediately, to the horror of the wretched fugitive, the lion himself appeared. The man gave himself up for lost. But, to his utter astonishment, the lion, instead of springing upon him and devouring him, came and fawned upon him, at the same time whining and lifting up his paw. Observing it to be much swollen and inflamed, he examined it and found a large thorn embedded in the ball of the foot. He accordingly removed it and dressed the wound as well as he could; and in course of time it healed up completely.

The lion's gratitude was unbounded. He looked upon the man as his friend, and they shared the cave for some time together. A day came, however, when the slave began to long for the society of his fellowmen, and he bade farewell to the lion and returned to the town. Here he was presently recognized and carried off in chains to his former master, who resolved to make an example of him, and ordered that he should be thrown to the beasts at the next public spectacle in the theater.

On the fatal day the beasts were loosed into the arena, and among the rest a lion of huge bulk and ferocious aspect. And then the wretched slave was cast in among them. What was the amazement of the spectators, when the lion after one glance bounded up to him and lay down at his feet with every expression of affection and delight! It was his old friend of the cave! The audience clamored that the slave's life should be spared; and the governor of the town, marveling at such gratitude and fidelity in a beast, decreed that both should receive their liberty.

THE FLEA AND THE MAN

## 39 . THE FLEA AND THE MAN

A flea bit a man, and bit him again, and again, till he could stand it no longer, but made a thorough search for it, and at last succeeded in catching it. Holding it between his finger and thumb, he said—or rather shouted, so angry was he—"Who are you, pray, you wretched little creature, that you make so free with my person?" The flea, terrified, whimpered in a weak little voice, "Oh, sir! Pray let me go. Don't kill me! I am such a little thing that I can't do you much harm." But the man laughed and said, "I am going to kill you now, at once. Whatever is bad has got to be destroyed, no matter how slight the harm it does."

**Do not waste your pity on a scamp.**

## 40. THE BEE AND JUPITER

A queen bee from Hymettus flew up to Olympus with some fresh honey from the hive as a present to Jupiter, who was so pleased with the gift that he promised to give her anything she liked to ask for. She said she would be very grateful if he would give stings to the bees, to kill people who robbed them of their honey. Jupiter was greatly displeased with this request, for he loved mankind. But he had given his word, so he said that stings they should have. The stings he gave them, however, were of such a kind that whenever a bee stings a man the sting is left in the wound, and the bee dies.

Evil wishes, like fowls, come home to roost.

## 41. THE OAK AND THE REEDS

An oak that grew on the bank of a river was uprooted by a severe gale of wind, and thrown across the stream. It fell among some reeds growing by the water, and said to them, "How is it that you, who are so frail and slender, have managed to weather the storm, whereas I, with all my strength, have been torn up by the roots and hurled into the river?" "You were stubborn," came the reply, "and fought against the storm, which proved stronger than you. But we bow and yield to every breeze, and thus the gale passed harmlessly over our heads."

**THE OAK AND THE REEDS**

## 42. THE BLIND MAN AND THE CUB

There was once a blind man who had so fine a sense of touch that when any animal was put into his hands he could tell what it was merely by the feel of it. One day the cub of a wolf was put into his hands, and he was asked what it was. He felt it for some time, and then said, "Indeed, I am not sure whether it is a wolf's cub or a fox's. But this I know: It would never do to trust it in a sheepfold."

**Evil tendencies are early shown.**

## 43. THE BOY AND THE SNAILS

A farmer's boy went looking for snails, and when he had picked up both his hands full he set about making a fire at which to roast them, for he meant to eat them. When it got well alight and the snails began to feel the heat, they gradually withdrew more and more into their shells with the hissing noise they always make when they do so. When the boy heard it, he said, "You abandoned creatures, how can you find heart to whistle when your houses are burning?"

## 44 · THE APES AND THE
## TWO TRAVELERS

———————

Two men were traveling together, one of whom never spoke the truth, whereas the other never told a lie; and they came in the course of their travels to the land of apes. The king of the apes, hearing of their arrival, ordered them to be brought before him; and by way of impressing them with his magnificence, he received them sitting on a throne, while the apes, his subjects, were ranged in long rows on either side of him. When the travelers came into his presence he asked them what they thought of him as a king. The lying traveler said, "Sire, everyone must see that you are a most noble and mighty monarch." "And what do you think of my subjects?" continued the king. "They," said the traveler, "are in every way worthy of their royal master." The ape was so delighted with his answer that he gave him a very handsome present.

The other traveler thought that if his companion was rewarded so splendidly for telling a lie, he himself would certainly receive a still greater reward for telling the truth. So when the ape turned to him and said, "And what, sir, is your opinion?" he replied, "I think you are a very fine ape, and all your subjects are fine apes too." The king of the apes was so enraged at his reply that he ordered him to be taken away and clawed to death.

## 45. THE ASS AND HIS BURDENS

A peddler who owned an ass one day bought a quantity of salt and loaded up his beast with as much as he could bear. On the way home the ass stumbled as he was crossing a stream and fell into the water. The salt got thoroughly wetted and much of it melted and drained away, so that, when he got on his legs again, the ass found his load had become much less heavy. His master, however, drove him back to town and bought more salt, which he added to what remained in the panniers, and started out again. No sooner had they reached a stream than the ass lay down in it, and rose, as before, with a much lighter load. But his master detected the trick and, turning back once more, bought a large number of sponges, and piled them on the back of the ass. When they came to the stream the ass again lay down. But this time, as the sponges soaked up large quantities of water, he found, when he got up on his legs that he had a bigger burden to carry than ever.

**You may play a good card once too often.**

## 46. THE SHEPHERD'S BOY
## AND THE WOLF

---

A shepherd's boy was tending his flock near a village, and thought it would be great fun to hoax the villagers by pretending that a wolf was attacking the sheep; so he shouted out, "Wolf! Wolf!" and when the people came running up he laughed at them for their pains. He did this more than once, and every time the villagers found they had been hoaxed, for there was no wolf at all. At last a wolf really did come, and the boy cried, "Wolf! Wolf!" as loud as he could. But the people were so used to hearing him call that they took no notice of his cries for help. And so the wolf had it all his own way, and killed off sheep after sheep at his leisure.

**You cannot believe a liar even when he tells the truth.**

## 47 . THE FOX AND THE GOAT

A fox fell into a well and was unable to get out again. By and by a thirsty goat came by, and seeing the fox in the well asked him if the water was good. "Good?" said the fox. "It's the best water I ever tasted in all my life. Come down and try it yourself." The goat thought of nothing but the prospect of quenching his thirst, and jumped in at once. When he had had enough to drink, he looked about, like the fox, for some way of getting out, but could find none.

Presently the fox said, "I have an idea. You stand on your hind legs and plant your forelegs firmly against the side of the well, and then I'll climb onto your back, and, from there, by stepping on your horns, I can get out. And when I'm out, I'll help you out too." The goat did as he was requested, and the fox climbed onto his back and so out of the well. And then he coolly walked away. The goat called loudly after him and reminded him of his promise to help him out. But the fox merely turned and said, "If you had as much sense in your head as you have hair in your beard you wouldn't have got into the well without making certain that you could get out again."

**Look before you leap.**

## 48. THE FISHERMAN AND THE SPRAT

A fisherman cast his net into the sea, and when he drew it up again it contained nothing but a single sprat that begged to be put back into the water. "I'm only a little fish now," it said, "but I shall grow big one day, and then if you come and catch me again I shall be of some use to you." But the fisherman replied, "Oh, no, I shall keep you now I've got you. If I put you back, should I ever see you again? Not likely!"

## 49 . THE BOASTING TRAVELER

A man once went abroad on his travels, and when he came home he had wonderful tales to tell of the things he had done in foreign countries. Among other things, he said he had taken part in a jumping match at Rhodes, and had done a wonderful jump which no one could beat. "Just go to Rhodes and ask them," he said. "Everyone will tell you it's true." But one of those who were listening said, "If you can jump as well as all that, we needn't go to Rhodes to prove it. Let's just imagine this is Rhodes for a minute; and now—jump!"

Deeds, not words.

## 50 . THE CRAB AND HIS MOTHER

An old crab said to her son, "Why do you walk sideways like that, my son? You ought to walk straight." The young crab replied, "Show me how, dear mother, and I'll follow your example." The old crab tried, but tried in vain, and then saw how foolish she had been to find fault with her child.

Example is better than precept.

**THE CRAB AND HIS MOTHER**

## 51. THE ASS AND HIS SHADOW

A certain man hired an ass for a journey in summertime, and started out with the owner following behind to drive the beast. By and by, in the heat of the day, they stopped to rest, and the traveler wanted to lie down in the ass's shadow. But the owner, who himself wished to be out of the sun, wouldn't let him do that; for he said he had hired the ass only, and not his shadow. The other maintained that his bargain secured him complete control of the ass for the time being. From words they came to blows. And while they were belaboring each other the ass took to his heels and was soon out of sight.

## 52. THE FARMER AND HIS SONS

A farmer, being at death's door and desiring to impart to his sons a secret of much moment, called them round him and said, "My sons, I am shortly about to die. I would have you know, therefore, that in my vineyard there lies a hidden treasure. Dig, and you will find it." As soon as their father was dead, the sons took spade and fork and turned up the soil of the vineyard over and over again, in their search for the treasure which they supposed to lie buried there. They found none, however; but the vines, after so thorough a digging, produced a crop such as had never before been seen.

## 53 · THE DOG AND THE COOK

A rich man once invited a number of his friends and acquaintances to a banquet. His dog thought it would be a good opportunity to invite another dog, a friend of his; so he went to him and said, "My master is giving a feast. There'll be a fine spread, so come and dine with me tonight." The dog thus invited came, and when he saw the preparations being made in the kitchen he said to himself, "My word, I'm in luck. I'll take care to eat enough tonight to last me two or three days." At the same time he wagged his tail briskly, by way of showing his friend how delighted he was to have been asked.

But just then the cook caught sight of him, and, in his annoyance at seeing a strange dog in the kitchen, caught him up by the hind legs and threw him out of the window. He had a nasty fall, and limped away as quickly as he could, howling dismally. Presently some other dogs met him and said, "Well, what sort of a dinner did you get?" To which he replied, "I had a splendid time. The wine was so good, and I drank so much of it, that I really don't remember how I got out of the house!"

**Be shy of favors bestowed at the expense of others.**

## 54. THE MONKEY AS KING

At a gathering of all the animals the monkey danced and delighted them so much that they made him their king. The fox, however, was very much disgusted at the promotion of the monkey. So having one day found a trap with a piece of meat in it, he took the monkey there and said to him, "Here is a dainty morsel I have found, sire; I did not take it myself, because I thought it ought to be reserved for you, our king. Will you be pleased to accept it?" The monkey made at once for the meat and got caught in the trap. Then he bitterly reproached the fox for leading him into danger. But the fox only laughed and said, "O monkey, you call yourself king of the beasts and haven't more sense than to be taken in like that!"

## 55. THE THIEVES AND THE COCK

Some thieves broke into a house and found nothing worth taking except a cock, which they seized and carried off with them. When they were preparing their supper, one of them caught up the cock, and was about to wring his neck, when he cried out for mercy and said, "Pray do not kill me. You will find me a most useful bird, for I rouse honest men to their work in the morning by my crowing." But the thief replied with some heat, "Yes, I know you do, making it still harder for us to get a livelihood. Into the pot you go!"

## 56. THE FARMER AND FORTUNE

A farmer was plowing one day on his farm when he turned up a pot of golden coins with his plow. He was overjoyed at his discovery and from that time forth made an offering daily at the shrine of the Goddess of the Earth. Fortune was displeased at this and came to him and said, "My man, why do you give Earth the credit for the gift which I bestowed upon you? You never thought of thanking me for your good luck. But should you be unlucky enough to lose what you have gained, I know very well that I, Fortune, should then come in for all the blame."

Show gratitude where gratitude is due.

## 57. JUPITER AND THE MONKEY

Jupiter issued a proclamation to all the beasts and offered a prize to the one who, in his judgment, produced the most beautiful offspring. Among the rest came the monkey, carrying a baby monkey in her arms, a hairless, flat-nosed little fright. When they saw it the gods all burst into peal on peal of laughter. But the monkey hugged her little one to her and said, "Jupiter may give the prize to whomsoever he likes, but I shall always think my baby the most beautiful of them all."

## 58. FATHER AND SONS

A certain man had several sons who were always quarreling with one another, and, try as he might, he could not get them to live together in harmony. So he determined to convince them of their folly by the following means. Bidding them fetch a bundle of sticks, he invited each in turn to break it across his knee. All tried and all failed. And then he undid the bundle and handed them the sticks one by one, when they had no difficulty at all in breaking them. "There, my boys," said he, "united you will be more than a match for your enemies. But if you quarrel and separate, your weakness will put you at the mercy of those who attack you."

Union is strength.

## 59. THE LAMP

A lamp, well filled with oil, burned with a clear and steady light, and began to swell with pride and boast that it shone more brightly than the sun himself. Just then a puff of wind came and blew it out. Someone struck a match and lit it again, and said, "You just keep alight, and never mind the sun. Why, even the stars never need to be relit as you had to be just now."

THE OWL AND THE BIRDS

## 60. THE OWL AND THE BIRDS

The owl is a very wise bird; and once, long ago, when the first oak sprouted in the forest, she called all the other birds together and said to them, "You see this tiny tree? If you take my advice, you will destroy it now when it is small; for when it grows big, the mistletoe will appear upon it, from which birdlime will be prepared for your destruction." Again, when the first flax was sown, she said to them, "Go and eat up that seed, for it is the seed of the flax, out of which men will one day make nets to catch you." Once more, when she saw the first archer, she warned the birds that he was their deadly enemy, who would wing his arrows with their own feathers and shoot them.

But they took no notice of what she said. In fact, they thought she was rather mad, and laughed at her. When, however, everything turned out as she had foretold, they changed their minds and conceived a great respect for her wisdom. Hence, whenever she appears, the birds attend upon her in the hope of hearing something that may be for their good. She, however, gives them advice no longer, but sits moping and pondering on the folly of her kind.

## 61. THE ASS IN THE LION'S SKIN

An ass found a lion's skin, and dressed himself up in it. Then he went about frightening everyone he met, for they all took him to be a lion, men and beasts alike, and took to their heels when they saw him coming. Elated by the success of his trick, he loudly brayed in triumph. The fox heard him, and recognized him at once for the ass he was, and said to him, "Oho, my friend, it's you, is it? I, too, should have been afraid if I hadn't heard your voice."

## 62. THE SHE-GOATS
## AND THEIR BEARDS

Jupiter granted beards to the she-goats at their own request, much to the disgust of the he-goats, who considered this to be an unwarrantable invasion of their rights and dignities. So they sent a deputation to him to protest against his action. He, however, advised them not to raise any objections. "What's in a tuft of hair?" said he. "Let them have it if they want it. They can never be a match for you in strength."

## 63 . THE OLD LION

A lion, enfeebled by age and no longer able to procure food for himself by force, determined to do so by cunning. Betaking himself to a cave, he lay down inside and feigned to be sick; and whenever any of the other animals entered to inquire after his health, he sprang upon them and devoured them. Many lost their lives in this way, till one day a fox called at the cave, and, having a suspicion of the truth, addressed the lion from outside instead of going in, and asked him how he did. He replied that he was in a very bad way. "But," said he, "why do you stand outside? Pray come in." "I should have done so," answered the fox, "if I hadn't noticed that all the footprints point towards the cave and none the other way."

## 64. THE BOY BATHING

A boy was bathing in a river and got out of his depth, and was in great danger of being drowned. A man who was passing along a road hard by heard his cries for help, and went to the riverside and began to scold him for being so careless as to get into deep water, but made no attempt to help him. "Oh, sir," cried the boy, "please help me first and scold me afterwards."

**Give assistance, not advice, in a crisis.**

THE QUACK FROG

## 65. THE QUACK FROG

Once upon a time a frog came forth from his home in the marshes and proclaimed to all the world that he was a learned physician, skilled in drugs and able to cure all diseases. Among the crowd was a fox, who called out, "You a doctor! Why, how can you set up to heal others when you cannot even cure your own lame legs and blotched and wrinkled skin?"

**Physician, heal thyself.**

## 66. THE SWOLLEN FOX

A hungry fox found in a hollow tree a quantity of bread and meat which some shepherds had placed there against their return. Delighted with his find he slipped in through the narrow aperture and greedily devoured it all. But when he tried to get out again he found himself so swollen after his big meal that he could not squeeze through the hole, and fell to whining and groaning over his misfortune. Another fox, happening to pass that way, came and asked him what the matter was; and, on learning the state of the case, said, "Well, my friend, I see nothing for it but for you stay where you are till you shrink to your former size. You'll get out then easily enough."

## 67. THE MOUSE, THE FROG, AND THE HAWK

A mouse and a frog struck up a friendship. They were not well mated, for the mouse lived entirely on land, while the frog was equally at home on land or in the water. In order that they might never be separated, the frog tied himself and the mouse together by the leg with a piece of thread. As long as they kept on dry land all went fairly well; but, coming to the edge of a pool, the frog jumped in, taking the mouse with him, and began swimming about and croaking with pleasure. The unhappy mouse, however, was soon drowned, and floated about on the surface in the wake of the frog. There he was spied by a hawk, who pounced down on him and seized him in his talons. The frog was unable to loose the knot which bound him to the mouse, and thus was carried off along with him and eaten by the hawk.

## 68. THE BOY AND THE NETTLES

A boy was gathering berries from a hedge when his hand was stung by a nettle. Smarting with the pain, he ran to tell his mother, and said to her between his sobs, "I only touched it ever so lightly, mother." "That's just why you got stung, my son," said she. "If you had grasped it firmly it wouldn't have hurt you in the least."

## 69 . THE PEASANT AND
## THE APPLE TREE

A peasant had an apple tree growing in his garden, which bore no fruit, but merely served to provide a shelter from the heat for the sparrows and grasshoppers which sat and chirped in its branches. Disappointed at its barrenness he determined to cut it down, and went and fetched his ax for the purpose. But when the sparrows and the grasshoppers saw what he was about to do, they begged him to spare it, and said to him, "If you destroy the tree we shall have to seek shelter elsewhere, and you will no longer have our merry chirping to enliven your work in the garden."

He, however, refused to listen to them, and set to work with a will to cut through the trunk. A few strokes showed that it was hollow inside and contained a swarm of bees and a large store of honey. Delighted with his find he threw down his ax, saying, "The old tree is worth keeping after all."

**Utility is most men's test of worth.**

## 70. THE JACKDAW AND THE PIGEONS

A jackdaw,* watching some pigeons in a farmyard, was filled with envy when he saw how well they were fed and determined to disguise himself as one of them, in order to secure a share of the good things they enjoyed. So he painted himself white from head to foot and joined the flock; and, so long as he was silent, they never suspected that he was not a pigeon like themselves.

But one day he was unwise enough to start chattering, when they at once saw through his disguise and pecked him so unmercifully that he was glad to escape and join his own kind again. But the other jackdaws did not recognize him in his white dress, and would not let him feed with them, but drove him away. And so he became a homeless wanderer for his pains.

## 71. JUPITER AND THE TORTOISE

Jupiter was about to marry a wife and determined to celebrate the event by inviting all the animals to a banquet. They all came except the tortoise, who did not put in an appearance, much to Jupiter's surprise. So when he next saw the tortoise he asked him why he had not been at the banquet. "I don't care for going out," said the tortoise. "There's no place like home." Jupiter was so much annoyed by this reply that he decreed that from that time forth the tortoise should carry his house upon his back, and never be able to get away from home even if he wished to.

---

*A common black and gray bird related to the crow.

## 72. THE DOG IN THE MANGER

A dog was lying in a manger on the hay which had been put there for the cattle, and when they came and tried to eat, he growled and snapped at them and wouldn't let them get at their food. "What a selfish beast," said one of them to his companions. "He can't eat himself and yet he won't let those eat who can."

## 73 · THE TWO BAGS

Every man carries two bags about with him, one in front and one behind, and both are packed full of faults. The bag in front contains his neighbors' faults, the one behind his own. Hence it is that men do not see their own faults, but never fail to see those of others.

## 74 · THE OXEN AND THE AXLETREES

A pair of oxen were drawing a heavily loaded wagon along the highway, and as they tugged and strained at the yoke the axletrees creaked and groaned terribly. This was too much for the oxen, who turned round indignantly and said, "Hullo, you there! Why do you make such a noise when we do all the work?"

**They complain most who suffer least.**

## 75 · THE BOY AND THE FILBERTS

A boy put his hand into a jar of filberts and grasped as many as his fist could possibly hold. But when he tried to pull it out again he found he couldn't do so, for the neck of the jar was too small to allow the passage of so large a handful. Unwilling to lose his nuts but unable to withdraw his hand, he burst into tears. A bystander, who saw where the trouble lay, said to him, "Come, my boy, don't be so greedy. Be content with half the amount, and you'll be able to get your hand out without difficulty."

**Do not attempt too much at once.**

# 76. THE FROGS ASKING FOR A KING

Time was when the frogs were discontented because they had no one to rule over them, so they sent a deputation to Jupiter to ask him to give them a king. Jupiter, despising the folly of their request, cast a log into the pool where they lived, and said that that should be their king. The frogs were terrified at first by the splash and scuttled away into the deepest parts of the pool.

But by and by, when they saw that the log remained motionless, one by one they ventured to the surface again, and before long, growing bolder, they began to feel such contempt for it that they even took to sitting upon it. Thinking that a king of that sort was an insult to their dignity, they sent to Jupiter a second time and begged him to take away the sluggish king he had given them and to give them another and a better one. Jupiter, annoyed at being pestered in this way, sent a stork to rule over them, who no sooner arrived among them than he began to catch and eat the frogs as fast as he could.

## 77 · THE OLIVE TREE AND
## THE FIG TREE

A n olive tree taunted a fig tree with the loss of her leaves at
a certain season of the year. "You," she said, "lose your leaves
every autumn and are bare till the spring; whereas I, as you
see, remain green and flourishing all the year round." Soon afterwards there came a heavy fall of snow, which settled on the leaves
of the olive so that she bent and broke under the weight. But the
flakes fell harmlessly through the bare branches of the fig, which
survived to bear many another crop.

## 78 · THE LION AND THE BOAR

O ne hot and thirsty day in the height of summer a lion and
a boar came down to a little spring at the same moment to
drink. In a trice they were quarreling as to who should drink
first. The quarrel soon became a fight, and they attacked one another
with utmost fury. Presently, stopping for a moment to take breath,
they saw some vultures seated on a rock above, evidently waiting for
one of them to be killed, when they would fly down and feed upon
the carcass. The sight sobered them at once, and they made up their
quarrel, saying, "We had much better be friends than fight and be
eaten by vultures."

## 79. THE WALNUT TREE

A walnut tree which grew by the roadside bore every year a plentiful crop of nuts. Everyone who passed by pelted its branches with sticks and stones in order to bring down the fruit, and the tree suffered severely. "It is hard," it cried, "that the very persons who enjoy my fruit should thus reward me with insults and blows."

## 80. THE MAN AND THE LION

A man and a lion were companions on a journey, and in the course of conversation they began to boast about their prowess, and each claimed to be superior to the other in strength and courage. They were still arguing with some heat when they came to a crossroad where there was a statue of a man strangling a lion. "There!" said the man triumphantly. "Look at that! Doesn't that prove to you that we are stronger than you?" "Not so fast, my friend," said the lion. "That is only your view of the case. If we lions could make statues, you may be sure that in most of them you would see the man underneath."

There are two sides to every question.

## 81. THE TORTOISE AND THE EAGLE

A tortoise, discontented with his lowly life and envious of the birds he saw disporting themselves in the air, begged an eagle to teach him to fly. The eagle protested that it was idle for him to try, as nature had not provided him with wings. But the tortoise pressed him with entreaties and promises of treasure, insisting that it could only be a question of learning the craft of the air. So at length the eagle consented to do the best he could for him and picked him up in his talons. Soaring with him to a great height in the sky, he then let him go, and the wretched tortoise fell headlong and was dashed to pieces on a rock.

## 82. THE KID ON THE HOUSETOP

A kid climbed up onto the roof of an outhouse, attracted by the grass and other things that grew in the thatch. And as he stood there browsing away he caught sight of a wolf passing below and jeered at him because he couldn't reach him. The wolf only looked up and said, "I hear you, my young friend. But it is not you who mock me, but the roof on which you are standing."

## 83. THE FOX WITHOUT A TAIL

Afox once fell into a trap and after a struggle managed to get free, but with the loss of his brush. He was then so much ashamed of his appearance that he thought life was not worth living unless he could persuade the other foxes to part with their tails also, and thus divert attention from his own loss. So he called a meeting of all the foxes and advised them to cut off their tails. "They're ugly things anyhow," he said, "and besides they're heavy, and it's tiresome to be always carrying them about with you." But one of the other foxes said, "My friend, if you hadn't lost your own tail you wouldn't be so keen on getting us to cut off ours."

## 84 . THE VAIN JACKDAW

Jupiter announced that he intended to appoint a king over the birds and named a day on which they were to appear before his throne, when he would select the most beautiful of them all to be their ruler. Wishing to look their best on the occasion they repaired to the banks of a stream, where they busied themselves in washing and preening their feathers.

The jackdaw was there along with the rest, and realized that with his ugly plumage he would have no chance of being chosen as he was. So he waited till they were all gone, and then picked up the most gaudy of the feathers they had dropped and fastened them about his own body, with the result that he looked gayer than any of them.

When the appointed day came, the birds assembled before Jupiter's throne; and, after passing them in review, he was about to make the jackdaw king, when all the rest set upon the king-elect, stripped him of his borrowed plumes, and exposed him for the jackdaw that he was.

## 85 . THE TRAVELER AND HIS DOG

A traveler was about to start on a journey and said to his dog, who was stretching himself by the door, "Come, what are you yawning for? Hurry up and get ready. I mean you to go with me." But the dog merely wagged his tail and said quietly, "I'm ready, master. It's you I'm waiting for."

## 86. THE SHIPWRECKED MAN
## AND THE SEA

A shipwrecked man cast up on the beach fell asleep after his struggle with the waves. When he woke up, he bitterly reproached the sea for its treachery in enticing men with its smooth and smiling surface, and then, when they were well embarked, turning in fury upon them and sending both ship and sailors to destruction. The sea arose in the form of a woman, and replied, "Lay not the blame on me, O sailor, but on the winds. By nature I am as calm and safe as the land itself, but the winds fall upon me with their gusts and gales, and lash me into a fury that is not natural to me."

## 87. THE WILD BOAR AND THE FOX

A wild boar was engaged in whetting his tusks upon the trunk of a tree in the forest when a fox came by and, seeing what he was at, said to him, "Why are you doing that, pray? The huntsmen are not out today, and there are no other dangers at hand that I can see." "True, my friend," replied the boar, "but the instant my life is in danger I shall need to use my tusks. There'll be no time to sharpen them then."

## 88. MERCURY AND THE SCULPTOR

Mercury was very anxious to know in what estimation he was held by mankind, so he disguised himself as a man and walked into a sculptor's studio where there were a number of statues finished and ready for sale. Seeing a statue of Jupiter among the rest, he inquired the price of it. "A crown," said the sculptor. "Is that all?" said he, laughing. "And (pointing to one of Juno) how much is that one?" "That," was the reply, "is half a crown." "And how much might you be wanting for that one over there, now?" he continued, pointing to a statue of himself. "That one?" said the sculptor. "Oh, I'll throw him in for nothing if you'll buy the other two."

## 89. THE FAWN AND HIS MOTHER

A hind said to her fawn, who was now well grown and strong, "My son, nature has given you a powerful body and a stout pair of horns, and I can't think why you are such a coward as to run away from the hounds." Just then they both heard the sound of a pack in full cry, but at a considerable distance. "You stay where you are," said the hind. "Never mind me." And with that she ran off as fast as her legs could carry her.

## 90. THE FOX AND THE LION

A fox who had never seen a lion one day met one, and was so terrified at the sight of him that he was ready to die with fear. After a time he met him again, and was still rather frightened, but not nearly so much as he had been when he met him first. But when he saw him for the third time he was so far from being afraid that he went up to him and began to talk to him as if he had known him all his life.

## 91. THE EAGLE AND HIS CAPTOR

A man once caught an eagle, and after clipping his wings turned him loose among the fowls in his henhouse, where he moped in a corner, looking very dejected and forlorn. After a while his captor was glad enough to sell him to a neighbor, who took him home and let his wings grow again. As soon as he had recovered the use of them, the eagle flew out and caught a hare, which he brought home and presented to his benefactor. A fox observed this, and said to the eagle, "Don't waste your gifts on him! Go and give them to the man who first caught you; make *him* your friend, and then perhaps he won't catch you and clip your wings a second time."

## 92. THE BLACKSMITH AND HIS DOG

A blacksmith had a little dog, which used to sleep when his master was at work, but was wide awake indeed when it was time for meals. One day his master pretended to be disgusted at this, and when he had thrown him a bone as usual, he said, "What on earth is the good of a lazy cur like you? When I am hammering away at my anvil, you just curl up and go to sleep; but no sooner do I stop for a mouthful of food than you wake up and wag your tail to be fed."

Those who will not work deserve to starve.

## 93. THE STAG AT THE POOL

A thirsty stag went down to a pool to drink. As he bent over the surface he saw his own reflection in the water, and was struck with admiration for his fine spreading antlers, but at the same time he felt nothing but disgust for the weakness and slenderness of his legs. While he stood there looking at himself, he was seen and attacked by a lion; but in the chase which ensued, he soon drew away from his pursuer, and kept his lead as long as the ground over which he ran was open and free of trees. But coming presently to a wood, he was caught by his antlers in the branches, and fell a victim to the teeth and claws of his enemy. "Woe is me!" he cried with his last breath. "I despised my legs, which might have saved my life. But I gloried in my horns, and they have proved my ruin."

**What is worth most is often valued least.**

## 94. THE DOG AND HIS REFLECTION

A dog was crossing a plank bridge over a stream with a piece of meat in his mouth, when he happened to see his own reflection in the water. He thought it was another dog with a piece of meat twice as big; so he let go his own, and flew at the other dog to get the other piece. But, of course, all that happened was that he got neither; for one was only a reflection, and the other was carried away by the current.

## 95. MERCURY AND THE TRADESMEN

When Jupiter was creating man, he told Mercury to make an infusion of lies, and to add a little of it to the other ingredients which went to the making of the tradesmen. Mercury did so, and introduced an equal amount into each in turn—the tallow chandler, and the greengrocer, and the haberdasher, and all, till he came to the horse dealer, who was last on the list, when, finding that he had a quantity of the infusion still left, he put it all into him. This is why all tradesmen lie more or less, but they none of them lie like a horse dealer.

## 96.  THE MICE AND THE WEASELS

There was war between the mice and the weasels, in which the mice always got the worst of it, numbers of them being killed and eaten by the weasels. So they called a council of war, in which an old mouse got up and said, "It's no wonder we are always beaten, for we have no generals to plan our battles and direct our movements in the field." Acting on his advice, they chose the biggest mice to be their leaders, and these, in order to be distinguished from the rank and file, provided themselves with helmets bearing large plumes of straw. They then led out the mice to battle, confident of victory; but they were defeated as usual, and were soon scampering as fast as they could to their holes. All made their way to safety without difficulty except the leaders, who were so hampered by the badges of their rank that they could not get into their holes, and fell easy victims to their pursuers.

**Greatness carries its own penalties.**

## 97 · THE PEACOCK AND JUNO

The peacock was greatly discontented because he had not a beautiful voice like the nightingale, and he went and complained to Juno about it. "The nightingale's song," said he, "is the envy of all the birds; but whenever I utter a sound I become a laughingstock." The goddess tried to console him by saying, "You have not, it is true, the power of song, but then you far excel all the rest in beauty. Your neck flashes like the emerald, and your splendid tail is a marvel of gorgeous color." But the peacock was not appeased. "What is the use," said he, "of being beautiful, with a voice like mine?" Then Juno replied, with a shade of sternness in her tones, "Fate has allotted to all their destined gifts: to yourself beauty, to the eagle strength, to the nightingale song, and so on to all the rest in their degree. But you alone are dissatisfied with your portion. Make, then, no more complaints, for if your present wish were granted, you would quickly find cause for fresh discontent."

THE BEAR AND THE FOX

## 98 . THE BEAR AND THE FOX

A bear was once bragging about his generous feelings, and saying how refined he was compared with other animals. (There is, in fact, a tradition that a bear will never touch a dead body.) A fox, who heard him talking in this strain, smiled and said, "My friend, when you are hungry, I only wish you would confine your attention to the dead and leave the living alone."

**A hypocrite deceives no one but himself.**

## 99 . THE ASS AND THE OLD PEASANT

A n old peasant was sitting in a meadow watching his ass, which was grazing close by, when all of a sudden he caught sight of armed men stealthily approaching. He jumped up in a moment, and begged the ass to fly with him as fast as he could, "Or else," said he, "we shall both be captured by the enemy." But the ass just looked round lazily and said, "And if so, do you think they'll make me carry heavier loads than I have to now?" "No," said his master. "Oh, well, then," said the ass, "I don't mind if they do take me, for I shan't be any worse off."

## 100. THE OX AND THE FROG

Two little frogs were playing about at the edge of a pool when an ox came down to the water to drink, and by accident trod on one of them and crushed the life out of him. When the old frog missed him, she asked his brother where he was. "He is dead, mother," said the little frog; "an enormous big creature with four legs came to our pool this morning and trampled him down in the mud." "Enormous, was he? Was he as big as this?" said the frog, puffing herself out to look as big as possible. "Oh! Yes, much bigger," was the answer. The frog puffed herself out still more. "Was he as big as this?" said she. "Oh! Yes, yes, mother, MUCH bigger," said the little frog. And yet again she puffed and puffed herself out till she was almost as round as a ball. "As big as . . . ?" she began—but then she burst.

# 101. THE MAN AND THE IMAGE

A poor man had a wooden image of a god, to which he used to pray daily for riches. He did this for a long time, but remained as poor as ever, till one day he caught up the image in disgust and hurled it with all his strength against the wall. The force of the blow split open the head, and a quantity of gold coins fell out upon the floor. The man gathered them up greedily, and said, "O you old fraud, you! When I honored you, you did me no good whatever; but no sooner do I treat you to insults and violence than you make a rich man of me!"

## 102. HERCULES AND THE WAGONER

A wagoner was driving his team along a muddy lane with a full load behind them, when the wheels of his wagon sank so deep in the mire that no efforts of his horses could move them. As he stood there, looking helplessly on, and calling loudly at intervals upon Hercules for assistance, the god himself appeared, and said to him, "Put your shoulder to the wheel, man, and goad on your horses, and then you may call on Hercules to assist you. If you won't lift a finger to help yourself, you can't expect Hercules or anyone else to come to your aid."

Heaven helps those who help themselves.

## 103 . THE POMEGRANATE, THE APPLE TREE, AND THE BRAMBLE

A pomegranate and an apple tree were disputing about the quality of their fruits, and each claimed that its own was the better of the two. High words passed between them, and a violent quarrel was imminent, when a bramble impudently poked its head out of a neighboring hedge and said, "There, that's enough, my friends. Don't let us quarrel." *

## 104 . THE LION, THE BEAR, AND THE FOX

A lion and a bear were fighting for possession of a kid, which they had both seized at the same moment. The battle was long and fierce, and at length both of them were exhausted, and lay upon the ground severely wounded and gasping for breath. A fox had all the time been prowling round and watching the fight, and when he saw the combatants lying there too weak to move, he slipped in and seized the kid and ran off with it. They looked on helplessly, and one said to the other, "Here we've been mauling each other all this while, and no one the better for it except the fox!"

---

*The significance here is that a lowly bramble would dare to interject himself into a dispute between two noble fruit trees.

## 105 . THE BLACKAMOOR

A man once bought an Ethiopian slave, who had black skin like all Ethiopians. But his new master thought his color was due to his late owner's having neglected him, and that all he wanted was a good scrubbing. So he set to work with plenty of soap and hot water, and rubbed away at him with a will, but all to no purpose. His skin remained as black as ever, while the poor wretch all but died from the cold he caught.

## 106 . THE TWO SOLDIERS
## AND THE ROBBER

Two soldiers traveling together were set upon by a robber. One of them ran away, but the other stood his ground, and laid about him so lustily with his sword that the robber was fain to fly and leave him in peace. When the coast was clear the timid one ran back, and, flourishing his weapon, cried in a threatening voice, "Where is he? Let me get at him, and I'll soon let him know whom he's got to deal with." But the other replied, "You are a little late, my friend. I only wish you had backed me up just now, even if you had done no more than speak, for I should have been encouraged, believing your words to be true. As it is, calm yourself, and put up your sword. There is no further use for it. You may delude others into thinking you're as brave as a lion; but I know that, at the first sign of danger, you run away like a hare."

## 107. THE LION AND THE WILD ASS

A lion and a wild ass went out hunting together. The latter was to run down the prey by his superior speed, and the former would then come up and dispatch it. They met with great success; and when it came to sharing the spoil the lion divided it all into three equal portions. "I will take the first," said he, "because I am king of the beasts; I will also take the second, because as your partner, I am entitled to half of what remains; and as for the third— well, unless you give it up to me and take yourself off pretty quick, the third, believe me, will make you feel very sorry for yourself!"

**Might makes right.**

## 108. THE MAN AND THE SATYR

A man and a satyr became friends and determined to live together. All went well for a while, until one day in wintertime
the satyr saw the man blowing on his hands. "Why do you
do that?" he asked. "To warm my hands," said the man. That same
day when they sat down to supper together, they each had a steam-
ing hot bowl of porridge, and the man raised his bowl to his mouth

and blew on it. "Why do you do that?" asked the satyr. "To cool my porridge," said the man. The satyr got up from the table. "Good-bye," said he, "I'm going. I can't be friends with a man who blows hot and cold with the same breath."

## 109. THE IMAGE SELLER

A certain man made a wooden image of Mercury, and exposed it for sale in the market. As no one offered to buy it, however, he thought he would try to attract a purchaser by proclaiming the virtues of the image. So he cried up and down the market, "A god for sale! A god for sale! One who'll bring you luck and keep you lucky!" Presently one of the bystanders stopped him and said, "If your god is all you make him out to be, how is it you don't keep him and make the most of him yourself?" "I'll tell you why," replied he. "He brings gain, it is true, but he takes his time about it; whereas I want money at once."

## 110. THE EAGLE AND THE ARROW

A n eagle sat perched on a lofty rock, keeping a sharp lookout for prey. A huntsman, concealed in a cleft of the mountain and on the watch for game, spied him there and shot an arrow at him. The shaft struck him full in the breast and pierced him through and through. As he lay in the agonies of death, he turned his eyes upon the arrow. "Ah, cruel fate!" he cried, "that I should perish thus. But oh, fate more cruel still, that the arrow which kills me should be winged with an eagle's feathers!"

## III. THE RICH MAN AND THE TANNER

A rich man took up his residence next door to a tanner, and found the smell of the tan yard so extremely unpleasant that he told him he must go. The tanner delayed his departure, and the rich man had to speak to him several times about it; and every time the tanner said he was making arrangements to move very shortly. This went on for some time, till at last the rich man got so used to the smell that he ceased to mind it, and troubled the tanner with his objections no more.

## 112. THE WOLF, THE MOTHER, AND HER CHILD

A hungry wolf was prowling about in search of food. By and by, attracted by the cries of a child, he came to a cottage. As he crouched beneath the window, he heard the mother say to the child, "Stop crying, do, or I'll throw you to the wolf!" Thinking she really meant what she said, he waited there a long time in the expectation of satisfying his hunger. In the evening he heard the mother fondling her child and saying, "If the naughty wolf comes, he shan't get my little one. Daddy will kill him." The wolf got up in much disgust and walked away. "As for the people in that house," said he to himself, "you can't believe a word they say."

## 113. THE OLD WOMAN AND
## THE WINE JAR

An old woman picked up an empty wine jar which had once contained a rare and costly wine, and which still retained some traces of its exquisite bouquet. She raised it to her nose and sniffed at it again and again. "Ah," she cried, "how delicious must have been the liquid which has left behind so ravishing a smell."

## 114. THE LIONESS AND THE VIXEN

A lioness and a vixen were talking together about their young, as mothers will, and saying how healthy and well grown they were, and what beautiful coats they had, and how they were the image of their parents. "My litter of cubs is a joy to see," said the fox. And then she added, rather maliciously, "But I notice you never have more than one." "No," said the lioness grimly, "but that one is a lion."

Quality, not quantity.

## 115. THE VIPER AND THE FILE

A viper entered a carpenter's shop, and went from one to another of the tools, begging for something to eat. Among the rest, he addressed himself to the file, and asked for the favor of a meal. The file replied in a tone of pitying contempt, "What a simpleton you must be if you imagine you will get anything from me, for I invariably take from everyone and never give anything in return."

The covetous are poor givers.

THE CAT AND THE COCK

## 116. THE CAT AND THE COCK

A cat pounced on a cock and cast about for some good excuse for making a meal off him, for cats don't as a rule eat cocks, and she knew she ought not to. At last she said, "You make a great nuisance of yourself at night by crowing and keeping people awake, so I am going to make an end of you." But the cock defended himself by saying that he crowed in order that men might wake up and set about the day's work in good time, and that they really couldn't very well do without him. "That may be," said the cat, "but whether they can or not, I'm not going without my dinner." And she killed and ate him.

The want of a good excuse never kept a villain from crime.

## 117. THE HARE AND THE TORTOISE

A hare was one day making fun of a tortoise for being so slow upon his feet. "Wait a bit," said the tortoise. "I'll run a race with you, and I'll wager that I win." "Oh, well," replied the hare, who was much amused at the idea, "let's try and see." And it was soon agreed that the fox should set a course for them and be the judge. When the time came both started off together, but the hare was soon so far ahead that he thought he might as well have a rest. So down he lay and fell fast asleep. Meanwhile the tortoise kept plodding on, and in time reached the goal. At last the hare woke up with a start and dashed on at his fastest, but only to find that the tortoise had already won the race.

**Slow and steady wins the race.**

## 118 . THE SOLDIER AND THE HORSE

A soldier gave his horse a plentiful supply of oats in time of war, and tended him with the utmost care, for he wished him to be strong to endure the hardships of the field, and swift to bear his master, when need arose, out of the reach of danger. But when the war was over he employed him on all sorts of drudgery, bestowing but little attention upon him, and giving him, moreover, nothing but chaff to eat. The time came when war broke out again, and the soldier saddled and bridled his horse, and, having put on his heavy coat of mail, mounted him to ride off and take the field. But the poor half-starved beast sank down under his weight, and said to his rider, "You will have to go into battle on foot this time. Thanks to hard work and bad food you have turned me from a horse into an ass; and you cannot in a moment turn me back again into a horse."

## 119 . THE OXEN AND THE BUTCHERS

Once upon a time the oxen determined to be revenged upon the butchers for the havoc they wrought in their ranks, and plotted to put them to death on a given day. They were all gathered together discussing how best to carry out the plan, and the more violent of them were engaged in sharpening their horns for the fray, when an old ox got up upon his feet and said, "My brothers, you have good reason, I know, to hate these butchers, but, at any rate, they understand their trade and do what they have to do without causing unnecessary pain. But if we kill them, others, who have no experience, will be set to slaughter us, and will by their bungling inflict great sufferings upon us. For you may be sure that even though all the butchers perish, mankind will never go without their beef."

## 120. THE WOLF AND THE LION

A wolf stole a lamb from the flock, and was carrying it off to devour it at his leisure when he met a lion, who took his prey away from him and walked off with it. He dared not resist, but when the lion had gone some distance he said, "It is most unjust of you to take what is mine away from me like that." The lion laughed and called out in reply, "It was justly yours, no doubt! The gift of a friend, perhaps, eh?"

## 121. THE SHEEP, THE WOLF, AND THE STAG

A stag once asked a sheep to lend him a measure of wheat, saying that his friend the wolf would be his surety. The sheep, however, was afraid that they meant to cheat her; so she excused herself, saying, "The wolf is in the habit of seizing what he wants and running off with it without paying, and you, too, can run much faster than I. So how shall I be able to come up with either of you when the debt falls due?"

**Two blacks do not make a white.**

## 122. THE LION AND THE THREE BULLS

Three bulls were grazing in a meadow, and were watched by a lion, who longed to capture and devour them, but who felt that he was no match for the three so long as they kept together. So he began by false whispers and malicious hints to foment jealousies and distrust among them. This stratagem succeeded so well that ere long the bulls grew cold and unfriendly, and finally avoided each other and fed each one by himself apart. No sooner did the lion see this than he fell upon them one by one and killed them in turn.

**The quarrels of friends are the opportunities of foes.**

## 123. THE HORSE AND HIS RIDER

A young man, who fancied himself something of a horseman, mounted a horse which had not been properly broken in and was exceedingly difficult to control. No sooner did the horse feel his weight in the saddle than he bolted, and nothing would stop him. A friend of the rider's met him in the road in his headlong career, and called out, "Where are you off to in such a hurry?" To which he, pointing to the horse, replied, "I've no idea. Ask him."

## 124. THE GOAT AND THE VINE

A goat was straying in a vineyard, and began to browse on the tender shoots of a vine which bore several fine bunches of grapes. "What have I done to you," said the vine, "that you should harm me thus? Isn't there grass enough for you to feed on? All the same, even if you eat up every leaf I have, and leave me quite bare, I shall produce wine enough to pour over you when you are led to the altar to be sacrificed."

THE TWO POTS

## 125. THE TWO POTS

Two pots, one of earthenware and the other of brass, were carried away down a river in flood. The brazen pot urged his companion to keep close by his side, and he would protect him. The other thanked him, but begged him not to come near him on any account. "For that," he said, "is just what I am most afraid of. One touch from you and I should be broken in pieces."

**Equals make the best friends.**

## 126. THE OLD HOUND

A hound who had served his master well for years, and had run down many a quarry in his time, began to lose his strength and speed owing to age. One day, when out hunting, his master started a powerful wild boar and set the hound at him. The latter seized the beast by the ear, but his teeth were gone and he could not retain his hold; so the boar escaped. His master began to scold him severely, but the hound interrupted him with these words, "My will is as strong as ever, master, but my body is old and feeble. You ought to honor me for what I have been instead of abusing me for what I am."

## 127. THE CLOWN AND
## THE COUNTRYMAN

A nobleman announced his intention of giving a public entertainment in the theater, and offered splendid prizes to all
who had any novelty to exhibit at the performance. The
announcement attracted a crowd of conjurers, jugglers, and acrobats,
and among the rest a clown, very popular with the crowd, who let
it be known that he was going to give an entirely new turn. When
the day of the performance came, the theater was filled from top to
bottom some time before the entertainment began. Several perform-
ers exhibited their tricks, and then the popular favorite came on
empty-handed and alone. At once there was a hush of expectation;
and he, letting his head fall upon his breast, imitated the squeak of
a pig to such perfection that the audience insisted on his producing
the animal, which, they said, he must have somewhere concealed
about his person. He, however, convinced them that there was no
pig there, and then the applause was deafening.

Among the spectators was a countryman, who disparaged the
clown's performance and announced that he would give a much
superior exhibition of the same trick on the following day. Again
the theater was filled to overflowing, and again the clown gave his
imitation amidst the cheers of the crowd. The countryman, meanwhile, before going on the stage, had secreted a young porker under
his smock; and when the spectators derisively bade him do better if
he could, he gave it a pinch in the ear and made it squeal loudly.
But they all with one voice shouted out that the clown's imitation
was much more true to life. Thereupon he produced the pig from
under his smock and said sarcastically, "There, that shows what sort
of judges you are!"

## 128. THE LARK AND THE FARMER

A lark nested in a field of corn, and was rearing her brood under cover of the ripening grain. One day, before the young were fully fledged, the farmer came to look at the crop, and, finding it yellowing fast, he said, "I must send round word to my neighbors to come and help me reap this field." One of the young larks overheard him, and was very much frightened, and asked her mother whether they hadn't better move house at once. "There's no hurry," replied she. "A man who looks to his friends for help will take his time about a thing." In a few days the farmer came by again, and saw that the grain was overripe and falling out of the ears upon the ground. "I must put it off no longer," he said. "This very day I'll hire the men and set them to work at once." The lark heard him and said to her young, "Come, my children, we must be off. He talks no more of his friends now, but is going to take things in hand himself."

**Self-help is the best help.**

## 129. THE LION AND THE ASS

A lion and an ass set up as partners and went a-hunting together. In course of time they came to a cave in which there were a number of wild goats. The lion took up his stand at the mouth of the cave and waited for them to come out, while the ass went inside and brayed for all he was worth in order to frighten them out into the open. The lion struck them down one by one as they appeared; and when the cave was empty the ass came out and said, "Well, I scared them pretty well, didn't I?" "I should think you did," said the lion. "Why, if I hadn't known you were an ass, I should have turned and run myself."

## 130. THE PROPHET

A prophet sat in the marketplace and told the fortunes of all who cared to engage his services. Suddenly there came running up one who told him that his house had been broken into by thieves, and that they had made off with everything they could lay hands on. He was up in a moment, and rushed off, tearing his hair and calling down curses on the miscreants. The bystanders were much amused, and one of them said, "Our friend professes to know what is going to happen to others, but it seems he's not clever enough to perceive what's in store for himself."

## 131. THE HOUND AND THE HARE

A young hound started a hare, and, when he caught her up, would at one moment snap at her with his teeth as though he were about to kill her, while at another he would let go his hold and frisk about her, as if he were playing with another dog. At last the hare said, "I wish you would show yourself in your true colors! If you are my friend, why do you bite me? If you are my enemy, why do you play with me?"

He is no friend who plays double.

## 132. THE LION, THE MOUSE, AND THE FOX

A lion was lying asleep at the mouth of his den when a mouse ran over his back and tickled him so that he woke up with a start and began looking about everywhere to see what it was that had disturbed him. A fox who was looking on thought he would have a joke at the expense of the lion, so he said, "Well, this is the first time I've seen a lion afraid of a mouse." "Afraid of a mouse?" said the lion testily. "Not I! It's his bad manners I can't stand."

## 133. THE TRUMPETER TAKEN PRISONER

A trumpeter marched into battle in the van of the army and put courage into his comrades by his warlike tunes. Being captured by the enemy, he begged for his life, and said, "Do not put me to death. I have killed no one. Indeed, I have no weapons, but carry with me only my trumpet here." But his captors replied, "That is only the more reason why we should take your life; for, though you do not fight yourself, you stir up others to do so."

THE WOLF AND THE CRANE

## 134. THE WOLF AND THE CRANE

A wolf once got a bone stuck in his throat. So he went to a crane and begged her to put her long bill down his throat and pull it out. "I'll make it worth your while," he added. The crane did as she was asked and got the bone out quite easily. The wolf thanked her warmly and was just turning away, when she cried, "What about that fee of mine?" "Well, what about it?" snapped the wolf, baring his teeth as he spoke. "You can go about boasting that you once put your head into a wolf's mouth and didn't get it bitten off. What more do you want?"

## 135. THE EAGLE, THE CAT,
## AND THE WILD SOW

An eagle built her nest at the top of a high tree; a cat with her family occupied a hollow in the trunk halfway down; and a wild sow and her young took up their quarters at the foot. They might have got on very well as neighbors had it not been for the evil cunning of the cat. Climbing up to the eagle's nest, she said to the eagle, "You and I are in the greatest possible danger. That dreadful creature, the sow, who is always to be seen grubbing away at the foot of the tree, means to uproot it, that she may devour your family and mine at her ease." Having thus driven the eagle almost out of her senses with terror, the cat climbed down the tree, and said to the sow, "I must warn you against that dreadful bird, the eagle. She is only waiting her chance to fly down and carry off one of your little pigs when you take them out, to feed her brood with." She succeeded in frightening the sow as much as the eagle. Then she returned to her hole in the trunk, from which, feigning to be afraid, she never came forth by day. Only by night did she creep out unseen to procure food for her kittens. The eagle meanwhile was afraid to stir from her nest, and the sow dared not leave her home among the roots; so that in time both they and their families perished of hunger, and their dead bodies supplied the cat with ample food for her growing family.

## 136. THE WOLF AND THE SHEEP

A wolf was worried and badly bitten by dogs, and lay a long time for dead. By and by he began to revive, and, feeling very hungry, called out to a passing sheep and said, "Would you kindly bring me some water from the stream close by? I can manage about meat, if only I could get something to drink." But this sheep was no fool. "I can quite understand," said he, "that if I brought you the water, you would have no difficulty about the meat. Good morning."

## 137 · THE TUNA FISH AND THE DOLPHIN

A tuna fish was chased by a dolphin and splashed through the water at a great rate, but the dolphin gradually gained upon him, and was just about to seize him when the force of his flight carried the tuna onto a sandbank. In the heat of the chase the dolphin followed him, and there they both lay out of the water, gasping for dear life.* When the tuna saw that his enemy was doomed like himself, he said, "I don't mind having to die now, for I see that he who is the cause of my death is about to share the same fate."

## 138 · THE THREE TRADESMEN

The citizens of a certain city were debating about the best material to use in the fortifications which were about to be erected for the greater security of the town. A carpenter got up and advised the use of wood, which he said was readily procurable and easily worked. A stone mason objected to wood on the ground that it was so inflammable, and recommended stones instead. Then a tanner got on his legs and said, "In my opinion there's nothing like leather."

**Every man for himself.**

---

*The ancient storyteller apparently did not know that dolphins are air-breathing mammals.

## 139 . THE MOUSE AND THE BULL

A bull gave chase to a mouse which had bitten him in the nose, but the mouse was too quick for him and slipped into a hole in a wall. The bull charged furiously into the wall again and again until he was tired out, and sank down on the ground exhausted with his efforts. When all was quiet, the mouse darted out and bit him again. Beside himself with rage, the bull started to his feet, but by that time the mouse was back in his hole again, and he could do nothing but bellow and fume in helpless anger. Presently he heard a shrill little voice say from inside the wall, "You big fellows don't always have it your own way. You see, sometimes we little ones come off best."

**The battle is not always to the strong.**

## 140. THE HARE AND THE HOUND

A hound started a hare from her form, and pursued her for some distance; but as she gradually gained upon him, he gave up the chase. A rustic who had seen the race met the hound as he was returning, and taunted him with his defeat. "The little one was too much for you," said he. "Ah, well," said the hound, "don't forget it's one thing to be running for your dinner, but quite another to be running for your life."

## 141. THE TOWN MOUSE AND

## THE COUNTRY MOUSE

A town mouse and a country mouse were acquaintances, and
the country mouse one day invited his friend to come and
see him at his home in the fields. The town mouse came,
and they sat down to a dinner of barleycorns and roots, the latter of
which had a distinctly earthy flavor. The fare was not much to the
taste of the guest, and presently he broke out with "My poor dear
friend, you live here no better than the ants. Now you should just
see how I fare! My larder is a regular horn of plenty. You must come
and stay with me, and I promise you, you shall live on the fat of the
land."

So when he returned to town he took the country mouse with
him and showed him into a larder containing flour and oatmeal and
figs and honey and dates. The country mouse had never seen anything like it, and sat down to enjoy the luxuries his friend provided.

But before they had well begun the door of the larder opened and someone came in. The two mice scampered off and hid themselves in a narrow and exceedingly uncomfortable hole. Presently, when all was quiet, they ventured out again; but someone else came in, and off they scuttled again. This was too much for the visitor. "Good-bye," said he, "I'm off. You live in the lap of luxury, I can see, but you are surrounded by dangers; whereas at home I can enjoy my simple dinner of roots and corn in peace."

## 142 . THE LION AND THE BULL

A lion saw a fine fat bull pasturing among a herd of cattle and cast about for some means of getting him into his clutches. So he sent him word that he was sacrificing a sheep, and asked if he would do him the honor of dining with him. The bull accepted the invitation, but, on arriving at the lion's den, he saw a great array of saucepans and spits, but no sign of a sheep; so he turned on his heel and walked quietly away. The lion called after him in an injured tone to ask the reason, and the bull turned round and said, "I have reason enough. When I saw all your preparations it struck me at once that the victim was to be a bull and not a sheep."

**The net is spread in vain in sight of the bird.**

THE WOLF, THE FOX, AND THE APE

## 143 . THE WOLF, THE FOX,
## AND THE APE

A wolf charged a fox with theft, which he denied, and the case was brought before an ape to be tried. When he had heard the evidence on both sides, the ape gave judgment as follows: "I do not think," he said, "that you, O wolf, ever lost what you claim. But all the same I believe that you, fox, are guilty of the theft, in spite of all your denials."

The dishonest get no credit, even if they act honestly.

## 144 . THE EAGLE AND THE COCKS

There were two cocks in the same farmyard, and they fought to decide who should be master. When the fight was over the beaten one went and hid himself in a dark corner, while the victor flew up onto the roof of the stables and crowed lustily. But an eagle espied him from high up in the sky, and swooped down and carried him off. Forthwith the other cock came out of his corner and ruled the roost without a rival.

Pride comes before a fall.

## 145. THE ESCAPED JACKDAW

A man caught a jackdaw and tied a piece of string to one of its legs, and then gave it to his children for a pet. But the jackdaw didn't at all like having to live with people; so, after a while, when he seemed to have become fairly tame, and they didn't watch him so closely, he slipped away and flew back to his old haunts. Unfortunately, the string was still on his leg, and before long it got entangled in the branches of a tree and the jackdaw couldn't get free, try as he would. He saw it was all up with him, and cried in despair, "Alas, in gaining my freedom I have lost my life."

## 146. THE FARMER AND THE FOX

A farmer was greatly annoyed by a fox, which came prowling about his yard at night and carried off his fowls. So he set a trap for him and caught him; and in order to be revenged upon him, he tied a bunch of tow to his tail and set fire to it and let him go. As ill luck would have it, however, the fox made straight for the fields where the corn was standing ripe and ready for cutting. It quickly caught fire and was all burnt up, and the farmer lost all his harvest.

**Revenge is a two-edged sword.**

## 147. VENUS AND THE CAT

A cat fell in love with a handsome young man, and begged the goddess Venus to change her into a woman. Venus was very gracious about it, and changed her at once into a beautiful maiden, whom the young man fell in love with at first sight and shortly afterwards married. One day Venus thought she would like to see whether the cat had changed her habits as well as her form, so she let a mouse run loose in the room where they were. Forgetting everything, the young woman had no sooner seen the mouse than up she jumped and was after it like a shot, at which the goddess was so disgusted that she changed her back again into a cat.

VENUS AND THE CAT

## 148. THE CROW AND THE SWAN

A crow was filled with envy on seeing the beautiful white plumage of a swan, and thought it was due to the water in which the swan constantly bathed and swam. So he left the neighborhood of the altars, where he got his living by picking up bits of the meat offered in sacrifice, and went and lived among the pools and streams. But though he bathed and washed his feathers many times a day, he didn't make them any whiter, and at last died of hunger into the bargain.

**You may change your habits, but not your nature.**

## 149 . THE STAG WITH ONE EYE

A stag, blind of one eye, was grazing close to the seashore and kept his sound eye turned towards the land, so as to be able to perceive the approach of the hounds, while the blind eye he turned towards the sea, never suspecting that any danger would threaten him from that quarter. As it fell out, however, some sailors, coasting along the shore, spied him and shot an arrow at him, by which he was mortally wounded. As he lay dying, he said to himself, "Wretch that I am! I bethought me of the dangers of the land, whence none assailed me; but I feared no peril from the sea, yet thence has come my ruin."

Misfortune often assails us from an unexpected quarter.

## 150 . THE FLY AND THE DRAFT MULE

A fly sat on one of the shafts of a cart and said to the mule who was pulling it, "How slow you are! Do mend your pace, or I shall have to use my sting as a goad." The mule was not in the least disturbed. "Behind me, in the cart," said he, "sits my master. He holds the reins, and flicks me with his whip, and him I obey, but I don't want any of your impertinence. I know when I may dawdle and when I may not."

THE COCK AND THE JEWEL

## 151. THE COCK AND THE JEWEL

A cock, scratching the ground for something to eat, turned up a jewel that had by chance been dropped there. "Ho!" said he. "A fine thing you are, no doubt, and, had your owner found you, great would his joy have been. But for me, give me a single grain of corn before all the jewels in the world!"

## 152. THE WOLF AND THE SHEPHERD

A wolf hung about near a flock of sheep for a long time, but made no attempt to molest them. The shepherd at first kept a sharp eye on him, for he naturally thought he meant mischief. But as time went by, and the wolf showed no inclination to meddle with the flock, he began to look upon him more as a protector than as an enemy; and when one day some errand took him to the city, he felt no uneasiness at leaving the wolf with the sheep. But as soon as his back was turned, the wolf attacked them and killed the greater number. When the shepherd returned and saw the havoc he had wrought, he cried, "It serves me right for trusting my flock to a wolf."

## 153 · THE FARMER AND THE STORK

A farmer set some traps in a field which he had lately sown with corn, in order to catch the cranes which came to pick up the seed. When he returned to look at his traps he found several cranes caught, and among them a stork, which begged to be let go, and said, "You ought not to kill me. I am not a crane, but a stork, as you can easily see by my feathers, and I am the most honest and harmless of birds." But the farmer replied, "It's nothing to me what you are. I find you among these cranes who ruin my crops, and, like them, you shall suffer."

If you choose bad companions, no one will believe that you are anything but bad yourself.

## 154 · THE CHARGER AND THE MILLER

A horse who had been used to carry his rider into battle felt himself growing old and chose to work in a mill instead. He now no longer found himself stepping out proudly to the beating of the drums, but was compelled to slave away all day grinding the corn. Bewailing his hard lot, he said one day to the miller, "Ah me! I was once a splendid war horse gaily caparisoned, and attended by a groom whose sole duty was to see to my wants. How different is my present condition! I wish I had never given up the battlefield for the mill." The miller replied with asperity, "It's no use your regretting the past. Fortune has many ups and downs. You must just take them as they come."

## 155 . THE GRASSHOPPER AND THE OWL

An owl who lived in a hollow tree was in the habit of feeding by night and sleeping by day, but her slumbers were greatly disturbed by the chirping of a grasshopper who had taken up his abode in the branches. She begged him repeatedly to have some consideration for her comfort, but the grasshopper, if anything, only chirped the louder. At last the owl could stand it no longer, but determined to rid herself of the pest by means of a trick. Addressing herself to the grasshopper, she said in her pleasantest manner, "As I cannot sleep for your song, which, believe me, is as sweet as the notes of Apollo's lyre, I have a mind to taste some nectar, which Minerva gave me the other day. Won't you come in and join me?" The grasshopper was flattered by the praise of his song, and his mouth, too, watered at the mention of the delicious drink, so he said he would be delighted. No sooner had he got inside the hollow where the owl was sitting than she pounced upon him and ate him up.

## 156. THE GRASSHOPPER AND
## THE ANTS

One fine day in winter some ants were busy drying their store of corn, which had got rather damp during a long spell of rain. Presently up came a grasshopper and begged them to spare her a few grains, "For," she said, "I'm simply starving." The ants stopped work for a moment, though this was against their principles. "May we ask," said they, "what you were doing with yourself all last summer? Why didn't you collect a store of food for the winter?" "The fact is," replied the grasshopper, "I was so busy singing that I hadn't the time." "If you spent the summer singing," replied the ants, "you can't do better than spend the winter dancing." And they chuckled and went on with their work.

## 157. THE FARMER AND THE VIPER

One winter a farmer found a viper frozen and numb with cold, and out of pity picked it up and placed it in his bosom. The viper was no sooner revived by the warmth than it turned upon its benefactor and inflicted a fatal bite upon him; and as the poor man lay dying, he cried, "I have only got what I deserved, for taking compassion on so villainous a creature."

**Kindness is thrown away upon the evil.**

## 158. THE TWO FROGS

Two frogs were neighbors. One lived in a marsh, where there was plenty of water, which frogs love; the other in a lane some distance away, where all the water to be had was that which lay in the ruts after rain. The marsh frog warned his friend and pressed him to come and live with him in the marsh, for he would find his quarters there far more comfortable and—what was still more important—more safe. But the other refused, saying that he could not bring himself to move from a place to which he had become accustomed. A few days afterwards a heavy wagon came down the lane, and he was crushed to death under the wheels.

## 159. THE COBBLER TURNED DOCTOR

A very unskillful cobbler, finding himself unable to make a living at his trade, gave up mending boots and took to doctoring instead. He gave out that he had the secret of a universal antidote against all poisons, and acquired no small reputation, thanks to his talent for puffing himself. One day, however, he fell very ill; and the king of the country bethought him that he would test the value of his remedy. Calling, therefore, for a cup, he poured out a dose of the antidote, and, under pretense of mixing poison with it, added a little water, and commanded him to drink it. Terrified by the fear of being poisoned, the cobbler confessed that he knew nothing about medicine, and that his antidote was worthless. Then the king summoned his subjects and addressed them as follows: "What folly could be greater than yours? Here is this cobbler to whom no one will send his boots to be mended, and yet you have not hesitated to entrust him with your lives!"

## 160. THE ASS, THE COCK, AND THE LION

An ass and a cock were in a cattle pen together. Presently a lion, who had been starving for days, came along and was just about to fall upon the ass and make a meal of him when the cock, rising to his full height and flapping his wings vigorously, uttered a tremendous crow. Now if there is one thing that frightens a lion, it is the crowing of a cock; and this one had no sooner heard the noise than he fled. The ass was mightily elated at this, and thought that if the lion couldn't face a cock, he would be still less likely to stand up to an ass; so he ran out and pursued him. But when the two had got well out of sight and hearing of the cock, the lion suddenly turned upon the ass and ate him up.

**False confidence often leads to disaster.**

## 161. THE BELLY AND THE MEMBERS

The members of the body once rebelled against the belly. "You," they said to the belly, "live in luxury and sloth, and never do a stroke of work; while we not only have to do all the hard work there is to be done, but are actually your slaves and have to minister to all your wants. Now, we will do so no longer, and you can shift for yourself for the future." They were as good as their word, and left the belly to starve. The result was just what might have been expected. The whole body soon began to fail, and the members and all shared in the general collapse. And then they saw too late how foolish they had been.

## 162. THE BALD MAN AND THE FLY

A fly settled on the head of a bald man and bit him. In his eagerness to kill it he hit himself a smart slap. But the fly escaped, and said to him in derision, "You tried to kill me for just one little bite. What will you do to yourself now for the heavy smack you have just given yourself?" "Oh, for that blow I bear no grudge," he replied, "for I never intended myself any harm; but as for you, you contemptible insect, who live by sucking human blood, I'd have borne a good deal more than that for the satisfaction of dashing the life out of you!"

## 163 . THE ASS AND THE WOLF

An ass was feeding in a meadow, and, catching sight of his enemy the wolf in the distance, pretended to be very lame and hobbled painfully along. When the wolf came up he asked the ass how he came to be so lame, and the ass replied that in going through a hedge he had trodden on a thorn, and he begged the wolf to pull it out with his teeth, "In case," he said, "when you eat me, it should stick in your throat and hurt you very much." The wolf said he would, and told the ass to lift up his foot, and gave his whole mind to getting out the thorn. But the ass suddenly let out with his heels and fetched the wolf a fearful kick in the mouth, breaking his teeth; and then he galloped off at full speed. As soon as he could speak the wolf growled to himself, "It serves me right. My father taught me to kill, and I ought to have stuck to that trade instead of attempting to cure."

## 164. THE MONKEY AND THE CAMEL

At a gathering of all the beasts the monkey gave an exhibition of dancing, and entertained the company vastly. There was great applause at the finish, which excited the envy of the camel and made him desire to win the favor of the assembly by the same means. So he got up from his place and began dancing, but he cut such a ridiculous figure as he plunged about, and made such a grotesque exhibition of his ungainly person, that the beasts all fell upon him with ridicule and drove him away.

## 165. THE SICK MAN AND THE DOCTOR

A sick man received a visit from his doctor, who asked him how he was. "Fairly well, doctor," said he, "but I find I sweat a great deal." "Ah," said the doctor, "that's a good sign." On his next visit he asked the same question, and his patient replied, "I'm much as usual, but I've taken to having shivering fits, which leave me cold all over." "Ah," said the doctor, "that's a good sign too." When he came the third time and inquired as before about his patient's health, the sick man said that he felt very feverish. "A very good sign," said the doctor; "you are doing very nicely indeed." Afterwards a friend came to see the invalid, and on asking him how he did, received this reply: "My dear friend, I'm dying of good signs."

THE TRAVELERS AND THE PLANE TREE

## 166. THE TRAVELERS AND
## THE PLANE TREE

Two travelers were walking along a bare and dusty road in the heat of a summer's day. Coming presently to a plane tree, they joyfully turned aside to shelter from the burning rays of the sun in the deep shade of its spreading branches. As they rested, looking up into the tree, one of them remarked to his companion, "What a useless tree the plane is! It bears no fruit and is of no service to man at all." The plane tree interrupted him with indignation. "You ungrateful creature," it cried, "you come and take shelter under me from the scorching sun, and then, in the very act of enjoying the cool shade of my foliage, you abuse me and call me good for nothing!"

**Many a service is met with ingratitude.**

## 167. THE FLEA AND THE OX

A flea once said to an ox, "How comes it that a big strong fellow like you is content to serve mankind, and do all their hard work for them, while I, who am no bigger than you see, live on their bodies and drink my fill of their blood, and never do a stroke for it all?" To which the ox replied, "Men are very kind to me, and so I am grateful to them. They feed and house me well, and every now and then they show their fondness for me by patting me on the head and neck." "They'd pat me, too," said the flea, "if I let them. But I take good care they don't, or there would be nothing left of me."

## 168. THE BIRDS, THE BEASTS, AND THE BAT

The birds were at war with the beasts, and many battles were fought with varying success on either side. The bat did not throw in his lot definitely with either party, but when things went well for the birds he was found fighting in their ranks; when, on the other hand, the beasts got the upper hand, he was to be found among the beasts. No one paid any attention to him while the war lasted. But when it was over, and peace was restored, neither the birds nor the beasts would have anything to do with so double-faced a traitor, and so he remains to this day a solitary outcast from both.

## 169. THE MAN AND HIS TWO MISTRESSES

A man of middle age, whose hair was turning grey, had two mistresses, an old woman and a young one. The elder of the two didn't like having a lover who looked so much younger than herself; so, whenever he came to see her, she used to pull the dark hairs out of his head to make him look old. The younger, on the other hand, didn't like him to look so much older than herself, and took every opportunity of pulling out the grey hairs, to make him look young. Between them, they left not a hair in his head, and he became perfectly bald.

## 170. THE EAGLE, THE JACKDAW, AND THE SHEPHERD

One day a jackdaw saw an eagle swoop down on a lamb and carry it off in its talons. "My word," said the jackdaw, "I'll do that myself." So it flew high up into the air, and then came shooting down with a great whirring of wings onto the back of a big ram. It had no sooner alighted than its claws got caught fast in the wool, and nothing it could do was of any use. There it stuck, flapping away, and only making things worse instead of better. By and by up came the shepherd. "Oho," he said. "So that's what you'd be doing, is it?" And he took the jackdaw, and clipped its wings and carried it home to his children. It looked so odd that they didn't know what to make of it. "What sort of bird is it, father?" they asked. "It's a jackdaw," he replied, "and nothing but a jackdaw. But it wants to be taken for an eagle."

If you attempt what is beyond your power, your trouble will be wasted and you court not only misfortune but ridicule.

## 171. THE WOLF AND THE BOY

A wolf, who had just enjoyed a good meal and was in a playful mood, caught sight of a boy lying flat upon the ground, and, realizing that he was trying to hide, and that it was fear of himself that made him do this, he went up to him and said, "Aha, I've found you, you see; but if you can say three things to me, the truth of which cannot be disputed, I will spare your life." The boy plucked up courage and thought for a moment, and then he said, "First, it is a pity you saw me; secondly, I was a fool to let myself be seen; and thirdly, we all hate wolves because they are always making unprovoked attacks upon our flocks." The wolf replied, "Well, what you say is true enough from your point of view; so you may go."

## 172. THE MILLER, HIS SON,
## AND THEIR ASS

A miller, accompanied by his young son, was driving his ass to market in hopes of finding a purchaser for him. On the road they met a troop of girls, laughing and talking, who exclaimed, "Did you ever see such a pair of fools? To be trudging along the dusty road when they might be riding!"

The miller thought there was sense in what they said; so he made his son mount the ass, and himself walked at the side. Presently they met some of his old cronies, who greeted them and said, "You'll spoil that son of yours, letting him ride while you toil along on foot! Make him walk, young lazybones! It'll do him all the good in the world."

The miller followed their advice, and took his son's place on the back of the ass, while the boy trudged along behind. They had not gone far when they overtook a party of women and children, and the miller heard them say, "What a selfish old man! He himself rides in comfort, but lets his poor little boy follow as best he can on his own legs!"

So he made his son get up behind him. Further along the road they met some travelers, who asked the miller whether the ass he was riding was his own property, or a beast hired for the occasion. He replied that it was his own, and that he was taking it to market to sell. "Good heavens!" said they. "With a load like that the poor beast will be so exhausted by the time he gets there that no one will look at him. Why, you'd do better to carry him!"

"Anything to please you," said the old man. "We can but try." So they got off, tied the ass's legs together with a rope and slung him on a pole, and at last reached the town, carrying him between them. This was so absurd a sight that the people ran out in crowds to laugh at it, and chaffed the father and son unmercifully, some even calling them lunatics. They had then got to a bridge over the river, where the ass, frightened by the noise and his unusual situation, kicked and struggled till he broke the ropes that bound him, and fell into the water and was drowned. Whereupon the unfortunate miller, vexed and ashamed, made the best of his way home again, convinced that in trying to please all, he had pleased none, and had lost his ass into the bargain.

## 173 · THE STAG AND THE VINE

A stag, pursued by the huntsmen, concealed himself under cover of a thick vine. They lost track of him and passed by his hiding place without being aware that he was anywhere near. Supposing all danger to be over, he presently began to browse on the leaves of the vine. The movement drew the attention of the returning huntsmen, and one of them, supposing some animal to be hidden there, shot an arrow at a venture into the foliage. The unlucky stag was pierced to the heart, and, as he expired, he said, "I deserve my fate for my treachery in feeding upon the leaves of my protector."

**Ingratitude sometimes brings its own punishment.**

## 174 · THE LAMB CHASED BY A WOLF

A wolf was chasing a lamb, which took refuge in a temple. The wolf urged it to come out of the precincts, and said, "If you don't, the priest is sure to catch you and offer you up in sacrifice on the altar." To which the lamb replied, "Thanks, I think I'll stay where I am. I'd rather be sacrificed any day than be eaten up by a wolf."

## 175. THE ARCHER AND THE LION

An archer went up into the hills to get some sport with his bow, and all the animals fled at the sight of him with the exception of the lion, who stayed behind and challenged him to fight. But he shot an arrow at the lion and hit him, and said, "There, you see what my messenger can do. Just you wait a moment and I'll tackle you myself." The lion, however, when he felt the sting of the arrow, ran away as fast as his legs could carry him. A fox, who had seen it all happen, said to the lion, "Come, don't be a coward. Why don't you stay and show fight?" But the lion replied, "You won't get me to stay, not you. Why, when he sends a messenger like that before him, he must himself be a terrible fellow to deal with."

Give a wide berth to those who can do damage at a distance.

**THE WOLF AND THE GOAT**

## 176 . THE WOLF AND THE GOAT

A wolf caught sight of a goat browsing above him on the scanty herbage that grew on the top of a steep rock; and being unable to get at her, tried to induce her to come lower down. "You are risking your life up there, madam, indeed you are," he called out. "Pray take my advice and come down here, where you will find plenty of better food." The goat turned a knowing eye upon him. "It's little you care whether I get good grass or bad," said she. "What you want is to eat me."

## 177 . THE SICK STAG

A stag fell sick and lay in a clearing in the forest, too weak to move from the spot. When the news of his illness spread, a number of the other beasts came to inquire after his health, and they one and all nibbled a little of the grass that grew round the invalid till at last there was not a blade within his reach. In a few days he began to mend, but was still too feeble to get up and go in search of fodder; and thus he perished miserably of hunger owing to the thoughtlessness of his friends.

## 178. THE ASS AND THE MULE

A certain man who had an ass and a mule loaded them both up one day and set out upon a journey. So long as the road was fairly level, the ass got on very well; but by and by they came to a place among the hills where the road was very rough and steep, and the ass was at his last gasp. So he begged the mule to relieve him of a part of his load, but the mule refused. At last, from sheer weariness, the ass stumbled and fell down a steep place and was killed. The driver was in despair, but he did the best he could. He added the ass's load to the mule's and he also flayed the ass and put his skin on the top of the double load. The mule could only just manage the extra weight, and, as he staggered painfully along, he said to himself, "I have only got what I deserved. If I had been willing to help the ass at first, I should not now be carrying his load and his skin into the bargain."

## 179. BROTHER AND SISTER

A certain man had two children, a boy and a girl; and the boy was as good-looking as the girl was plain. One day, as they were playing together in their mother's chamber, they chanced upon a mirror and saw their own features for the first time. The boy saw what a handsome fellow he was, and began to boast to his sister about his good looks. She, on her part, was ready to cry with vexation when she was aware of her plainness, and took his remarks as an insult to herself. Running to her father, she told him of her brother's conceit, and accused him of meddling with his mother's things. He laughed and kissed them both, and said, "My children, learn from now onwards to make a good use of the glass. You, my boy, strive to be as good as it shows you to be handsome; and you, my girl, resolve to make up for the plainness of your features by the sweetness of your disposition."

## 180. THE HEIFER AND THE OX

A heifer went up to an ox, who was straining hard at the plow, and sympathized with him in a rather patronizing sort of way on the necessity of his having to work so hard. Not long afterwards there was a festival in the village and everyone kept holiday. But, whereas the ox was turned loose into the pasture, the heifer was seized and led off to sacrifice. "Ah," said the ox, with a grim smile, "I see now why you were allowed to have such an idle time. It was because you were always intended for the altar."

## 181. THE KINGDOM OF THE LION

When the lion reigned over the beasts of the earth he was never cruel or tyrannical, but as gentle and just as a king ought to be. During his reign he called a general assembly of the beasts and drew up a code of laws under which all were to live in perfect equality and harmony. The wolf and the lamb, the tiger and the stag, the leopard and the kid, the dog and the hare, all should dwell side by side in unbroken peace and friendship. The hare said, "Oh! How I have longed for this day when the weak take their place without fear by the side of the strong!"

## 182. THE ASS AND HIS DRIVER

An ass was being driven down a mountain road, and after jogging along for a while sensibly enough he suddenly quitted the track and rushed to the edge of a precipice. He was just about to leap over the edge when his driver caught hold of his tail and did his best to pull him back. But pull as he might he couldn't get the ass to budge from the brink. At last he gave up, crying, "All right, then, get to the bottom your own way; but it's the way to sudden death, as you'll find out quick enough."

## 183. THE LION AND THE HARE

A lion found a hare sleeping in her form and was just going to devour her when he caught sight of a passing stag. Dropping the hare, he at once made for the bigger game; but finding, after a long chase, that he could not overtake the stag, he abandoned the attempt and came back for the hare. When he reached the spot, however, he found she was nowhere to be seen, and he had to go without his dinner. "It serves me right," he said. "I should have been content with what I had got, instead of hankering after a better prize."

## 184 . THE WOLVES AND THE DOGS

Once upon a time the wolves said to the dogs, "Why should we continue to be enemies any longer? You are very like us in most ways. The main difference between us is one of training only. We live a life of freedom; but you are enslaved to mankind, who beat you, and put heavy collars round your necks, and compel you to keep watch over their flocks and herds for them, and, to crown all, they give you nothing but bones to eat. Don't put up with it any longer, but hand over the flocks to us, and we will all live on the fat of the land and feast together." The dogs allowed themselves to be persuaded by these words, and accompanied the wolves into their den. But no sooner were they well inside than the wolves set upon them and tore them to pieces.

**Traitors richly deserve their fate.**

## 185 . THE BULL AND THE CALF

A full-grown bull was struggling to force his huge bulk through the narrow entrance to a cow house where his stall was, when a young calf came up and said to him, "If you'll step aside a moment, I'll show you the way to get through." The bull turned upon him an amused look. "I knew that way," said he, "before you were born."

THE TREES AND THE AX

## 186. THE TREES AND THE AX

A woodman went into the forest and begged of the trees the favor of a handle for his ax. The principal trees at once agreed to so modest a request, and unhesitatingly gave him a young ash sapling, out of which he fashioned the handle he desired. No sooner had he done so than he set to work to fell the noblest trees in the wood. When they saw the use to which he was putting their gift, they cried, "Alas! Alas! We are undone, but we are ourselves to blame. The little we gave has cost us all. Had we not sacrificed the rights of the ash, we might ourselves have stood for ages."

## 187. THE ASTRONOMER

There was once an astronomer whose habit it was to go out at night and observe the stars. One night, as he was walking about outside the town gates, gazing up absorbed into the sky and not looking where he was going, he fell into a dry well. As he lay there groaning, someone passing by heard him, and, coming to the edge of the well, looked down and, on learning what had happened, said, "If you really mean to say that you were looking so hard at the sky that you didn't even see where your feet were carrying you along the ground, it appears to me that you deserve all you've got."

## 188. THE LABORER AND THE SNAKE

A laborer's little son was bitten by a snake and died of the wound. The father was beside himself with grief, and in his anger against the snake he caught up an ax and went and stood close to the snake's hole, and watched for a chance of killing it. Presently the snake came out, and the man aimed a blow at it, but only succeeded in cutting off the tip of its tail before it wriggled in again. He then tried to get it to come out a second time, pretending that he wished to make up the quarrel. But the snake said, "I can never be your friend because of my lost tail, nor you mine because of your lost child."

**Injuries are never forgotten in the presence of those who caused them.**

## 189. THE CAGED BIRD AND THE BAT

A songbird was confined in a cage which hung outside a window, and had a way of singing at night when all other birds were asleep. One night a bat came and clung to the bars of the cage, and asked the bird why she was silent by day and sang only at night. "I have a very good reason for doing so," said the bird. "It was once when I was singing in the daytime that a fowler was attracted by my voice, and set his nets for me and caught me. Since then I have never sung except by night." But the bat replied, "It is no use your doing that now when you are a prisoner. If only you had done so before you were caught, you might still have been free."

**Precautions are useless after the event.**

## 190. THE ASS AND HIS PURCHASER

A man who wanted to buy an ass went to market, and, coming across a likely-looking beast, arranged with the owner that he should be allowed to take him home on trial to see what he was like. When he reached home he put him into his stable along with the other asses. The newcomer took a look round, and immediately went and chose a place next to the laziest and greediest beast in the stable. When the master saw this he put a halter on him at once, and led him off and handed him over to his owner again. The latter was a good deal surprised to see him back so soon, and said, "Why, do you mean to say you have tested him already?" "I don't want to put him through any more tests," replied the other. "I could see what sort of beast he is from the companion he chose for himself."

**A man is known by the company he keeps.**

## 191. THE KID AND THE WOLF

A kid strayed from the flock and was chased by a wolf. When he saw he must be caught he turned round and said to the wolf, "I know, sir, that I can't escape being eaten by you; and so, as my life is bound to be short, I pray you let it be as merry as may be. Will you not play me a tune to dance to before I die?" The wolf saw no objection to having some music before his dinner; so he took out his pipe and began to play, while the kid danced before him. Before many minutes were passed the gods who guarded the flock heard the sound and came up to see what was going on. They no sooner clapped eyes on the wolf than they gave chase and drove him away. As he ran off, he turned and said to the kid, "It's what I thoroughly deserve. My trade is the butcher's, and I had no business to turn piper to please you."

## 192. THE DEBTOR AND HIS SOW

A man of Athens fell into debt and was pressed for the money by his creditor; but he had no means of paying at the time, so he begged for delay. But the creditor refused and said he must pay at once. Then the debtor fetched a sow—the only one he had—and took her to market to offer her for sale. It happened that his creditor was there too. Presently a buyer came along and asked if the sow produced good litters. "Yes," said the debtor, "very fine ones; and the remarkable thing is that she produces females at the Mysteries and males at the Panathenea." (Festivals these were; and the Athenians always sacrifice a sow at one, and a boar at the other; while at the Dionysia they sacrifice a kid.) At that the creditor, who was standing by, put in, "Don't be surprised, sir. Why, still better, at the Dionysia this sow has kids!"

## 193. THE BALD HUNTSMAN

A man who had lost all his hair took to wearing a wig, and one day he went out hunting. It was blowing rather hard at the time, and he hadn't gone far before a gust of wind caught his hat and carried it off, and his wig too, much to the amusement of the hunt. But he quite entered into the joke, and said, "Ah, well! The hair that wig is made of didn't stick to the head on which it grew, so it's no wonder it won't stick to mine."

## 194. THE HERDSMAN AND
## THE LOST BULL

A herdsman was tending his cattle when he missed a young bull, one of the finest of the herd. He went at once to look for him, but, meeting with no success in his search, he made a vow, that if he should discover the thief he would sacrifice a calf to Jupiter. Continuing his search, he entered a thicket, where he presently espied a lion devouring the lost bull. Terrified with fear, he raised his hands to heaven and cried, "Great Jupiter, I vowed I would sacrifice a calf to thee if I should discover the thief; but now a full-grown bull I promise thee if only I myself escape unhurt from his clutches."

## 195. THE HOUND AND THE FOX

A hound, roaming in the forest, spied a lion, and being well used to lesser game, gave chase, thinking he would make a fine quarry. Presently the lion perceived that he was being pursued; so, stopping short, he rounded on his pursuer and gave a loud roar. The hound immediately turned tail and fled. A fox, seeing him running away, jeered at him and said, "Ho! Ho! There goes the coward who chased a lion and ran away the moment he roared!"

## 196. THE MULE

One morning a mule, who had too much to eat and too little to do, began to think himself a very fine fellow indeed, and frisked about saying, "My father was undoubtedly a high-spirited horse and I take after him entirely." But very soon afterwards he was put into the harness and compelled to go a very long way with a heavy load behind him. At the end of the day, exhausted by his unusual exertions, he said dejectedly to himself, "I must have been mistaken about my father; he can only have been an ass after all."

## 197. THE FATHER AND HIS DAUGHTERS

A man had two daughters, one of whom he gave in marriage to a gardener, and the other to a potter. After a time he thought he would go and see how they were getting on; and first he went to the gardener's wife. He asked her how she was and how things were going with herself and her husband. She replied that on the whole they were doing very well. "But," she continued, "I do wish we could have some good rain. The garden wants it badly." Then he went on to the potter's wife and made the same inquiries of her. She replied that she and her husband had nothing to complain of. "But," she went on, "I do wish we could have some nice dry weather, to dry the pottery." Her father looked at her with a humorous expression on his face. "You want dry weather," he said, "and your sister wants rain. I was going to ask in my prayers that your wishes should be granted; but now it strikes me I had better not refer to the subject."

## 198. THE THIEF AND THE INNKEEPER

A thief hired a room at an inn and stayed there some days on the lookout for something to steal. No opportunity, however, presented itself, till one day, when there was a festival to be celebrated, the innkeeper appeared in a fine new coat and sat down before the door of the inn for an airing. The thief no sooner set eyes upon the coat than he longed to get possession of it. There was no business doing, so he went and took a seat by the side of the innkeeper and began talking to him. They conversed together for some time, and then the thief suddenly yawned and howled like a wolf. The innkeeper asked him in some concern what ailed him. The thief replied, "I will tell you about myself, sir, but first I must beg you to take charge of my clothes for me, for I intend to leave them with you. Why I have these fits of yawning I cannot tell. Maybe they are sent as a punishment for my misdeeds; but, whatever the reason, the facts are that when I have yawned three times I become a ravening wolf and fly at men's throats." As he finished speaking he yawned a second time and howled again as before. The innkeeper, believing every word he said, and terrified at the prospect of being confronted with a wolf, got up hastily and started to run indoors; but the thief caught him by the coat and tried to stop him, crying, "Stay, sir, stay, and take charge of my clothes, or else I shall never see them again." As he spoke he opened his mouth and began to yawn for the third time. The innkeeper, mad with the fear of being eaten by a wolf, slipped out of his coat, which remained in the other's hands, and bolted into the inn and locked the door behind him; and the thief then quietly stole off with his spoil.

## 199. THE PACK ASS AND
## THE WILD ASS

A wild ass, who was wandering idly about, one day came upon a pack ass lying at full length in a sunny spot and thoroughly enjoying himself. Going up to him, he said, "What a lucky beast you are! Your sleek coat shows how well you live. How I envy you!" Not long after the wild ass saw his acquaintance again, but this time he was carrying a heavy load, and his driver was following behind and beating him with a thick stick. "Ah, my friend," said the wild ass, "I don't envy you anymore; for I see you pay dear for your comforts."

**Advantages that are dearly bought are doubtful blessings.**

## 200. THE ASS AND HIS MASTERS

A gardener had an ass which had a very hard time of it, what with scanty food, heavy loads, and constant beating. The ass therefore begged Jupiter to take him away from the gardener and hand him over to another master. So Jupiter sent Mercury to the gardener to bid him sell the ass to a potter, which he did. But the ass was as discontented as ever, for he had to work harder than before; so he begged Jupiter for relief a second time, and Jupiter very obligingly arranged that he should be sold to a tanner. But when the ass saw what his new master's trade was, he cried in despair,

"Why wasn't I content to serve either of my former masters, hard as I had to work and badly as I was treated? For they would have buried me decently, but now I shall come in the end to the tanning vat."

Servants don't know a good master till they have served a worse.

## 201. THE PACK ASS, THE WILD ASS, AND THE LION

A wild ass saw a pack ass, jogging along under a heavy load, and taunted him with the condition of slavery in which he lived, in these words: "What a vile lot is yours compared with mine! I am free as the air, and never do a stroke of work; and, as for fodder, I have only to go to the hills and there I find far more than enough for my needs. But you! You depend on your master for food, and he makes you carry heavy loads every day and beats you unmercifully." At that moment a lion appeared on the scene, and made no attempt to molest the pack ass, owing to the presence of the driver; but he fell upon the wild ass, who had no one to protect him, and without more ado made a meal of him.

It is no use being your own master unless you can stand up for yourself.

## 202. THE ANT

Ants were once men and made their living by tilling the soil. But, not content with the results of their own work, they were always casting longing eyes upon the crops and fruits of their neighbors, which they stole, whenever they got the chance, and added to their own store. At last their covetousness made Jupiter so angry that he changed them into ants. But, though their forms were changed, their nature remained the same; and so, to this day, they go about among the cornfields and gather the fruits of others' labor, and store them up for their own use.

**You may punish a thief, but his bent remains.**

## 203 . THE FROGS AND THE WELL

Two frogs lived together in a marsh. But one hot summer the marsh dried up, and they left it to look for another place to live in, for frogs like damp places if they can get them. By and by they came to a deep well, and one of them looked down into it and said to the other, "This looks a nice cool place. Let us jump in and settle here." But the other, who had a wiser head on his shoulders, replied, "Not so fast, my friend. Supposing this well dried up like the marsh, how should we get out again?"

**Think twice before you act.**

## 204 . THE CRAB AND THE FOX

A crab once left the seashore and went and settled in a meadow some way inland, which looked very nice and green and seemed likely to be a good place to feed in. But a hungry fox came along and spied the crab and caught him. Just as he was going to be eaten up, the crab said, "This is just what I deserve, for I had no business to leave my natural home by the sea and settle here as though I belonged to the land."

**Be content with your lot.**

THE FROGS AND THE WELL

## 205. THE FOX AND THE GRASSHOPPER

A grasshopper sat chirping in the branches of a tree. A fox heard her, and, thinking what a dainty morsel she would make, he tried to get her down by a trick. Standing below in full view of her, he praised her song in the most flattering terms, and begged her to descend, saying he would like to make the acquaintance of the owner of so beautiful a voice. But she was not to be taken in, and replied, "You are very much mistaken, my dear sir, if you imagine I am going to come down. I keep well out of the way of you and your kind ever since the day when I saw numbers of grasshoppers' wings strewn about the entrance to a fox's earth."

## 206. THE FARMER, HIS BOY, AND THE ROOKS

A farmer had just sown a field of wheat, and was keeping a careful watch over it, for numbers of rooks and starlings kept continually settling on it and eating up the grain. Along with him went his boy, carrying a sling; and whenever the farmer asked for the sling the starlings understood what he said and warned the rooks, and they were off in a moment. So the farmer hit on a trick. "My lad," said he, "we must get the better of these birds somehow. After this, when I want the sling, I won't say 'sling,' but just 'humph!' and you must then hand me the sling quickly."

Presently back came the whole flock. "Humph!" said the farmer;

but the starlings took no notice, and he had time to sling several stones among them, hitting one on the head, another in the legs, and another in the wing, before they got out of range. As they made all haste away they met some cranes, who asked them what the matter was. "Matter?" said one of the rooks. "It's those rascals, men, that are the matter. Don't you go near them. They have a way of saying one thing and meaning another, which has just been the death of several of our poor friends."

## 207. THE ASS AND THE DOG

An ass and a dog were on their travels together, and, as they went along, they found a sealed packet lying on the ground. The ass picked it up, broke the seal, and found it contained some writing, which he proceeded to read out aloud to the dog. As he read on, it turned out to be all about grass and barley and hay—in short, all the kinds of fodder that asses are fond of. The dog was a good deal bored with listening to all this, till at last his impatience got the better of him, and he cried, "Just skip a few pages, friend, and see if there isn't something about meat and bones." The ass glanced all through the packet, but found nothing of the sort, and said so. Then the dog said in disgust, "Oh, throw it away, do. What's the good of a thing like that?"

## 208. THE ASS CARRYING THE IMAGE

A certain man put an image on the back of his ass to take it to one of the temples of the town. As they went along the road all the people they met uncovered and bowed their heads out of reverence for the image; but the ass thought they were doing it out of respect for himself, and began to give himself airs accordingly. At last he became so conceited that he imagined he could do as he liked, and, by way of protest against the load he was carrying, he came to a full stop and flatly declined to proceed any further. His driver, finding him so obstinate, hit him hard and long with his stick, saying the while, "Oh, you dunderheaded idiot, do you suppose it's come to this, that men pay worship to an ass?"

**Rude shocks await those who take to themselves the credit that is due to others.**

## 209. THE ATHENIAN AND
## THE THEBAN

An Athenian and a Theban were on the road together and passed the time in conversation, as is the way of travelers. After discussing a variety of subjects they began to talk about heroes, a topic that tends to be more fertile than edifying. Each of them was lavish in his praises of the heroes of his own city, until eventually the Theban asserted that Hercules was the greatest hero who had ever lived on earth, and now occupied a foremost place among the gods; while the Athenian insisted that Theseus was far superior, for his fortune had been in every way supremely blessed, whereas Hercules had at one time been forced to act as a servant. And he gained his point, for he was a very glib fellow, like all Athenians; so that the Theban, who was no match for him in talking, cried at last in some disgust, "All right, have your way. I only hope that when our heroes are angry with us, Athens may suffer from the anger of Hercules, and Thebes only from that of Theseus."

THE GOATHERD AND THE GOAT

## 210. THE GOATHERD AND THE GOAT

A goatherd was one day gathering his flock to return to the fold, when one of his goats strayed and refused to join the rest. He tried for a long time to get her to return by calling and whistling to her, but the goat took no notice of him at all; so at last he threw a stone at her and broke one of her horns. In dismay, he begged her not to tell his master. But she replied, "You silly fellow, my horn would cry aloud even if I held my tongue."

**It's no use trying to hide what can't be hidden.**

## 211. THE SHEEP AND THE DOG

Once upon a time the sheep complained to the shepherd about the difference in his treatment of themselves and his dog. "Your conduct," said they, "is very strange and, we think, very unfair. We provide you with wool and lambs and milk, and you give us nothing but grass, and even that we have to find for ourselves. But you get nothing at all from the dog, and yet you feed him with tidbits from your own table." Their remarks were overheard by the dog, who spoke up at once and said, "Yes, and quite right, too. Where would you be if it wasn't for me? Thieves would steal you! Wolves would eat you! Indeed, if I didn't keep constant watch over you, you would be too terrified even to graze!" The sheep were obliged to acknowledge that he spoke the truth, and never again made a grievance of the regard in which he was held by his master.

## 212. THE SHEPHERD AND THE WOLF

A shepherd found a wolf's cub straying in the pastures, and took him home and reared him along with his dogs. When the cub grew to his full size, if ever a wolf stole a sheep from the flock, he used to join the dogs in hunting him down. It sometimes happened that the dogs failed to come up with the thief, and, abandoning the pursuit, returned home. The wolf would on such occasions continue the chase by himself, and when he overtook the culprit, would stop and share the feast with him, and then return to the shepherd. But if some time passed without a sheep being carried off by the wolves, he would steal one himself and share his plunder with the dogs. The shepherd's suspicions were aroused, and one day he caught him in the act; and, fastening a rope round his neck, hung him on the nearest tree.

What's bred in the bone is sure to come out in the flesh.

## 213. THE LION, JUPITER, AND THE ELEPHANT

The lion, for all his size and strength and his sharp teeth and claws, is a coward in one thing. He can't bear the sound of a cock crowing, and runs away whenever he hears it. He complained bitterly to Jupiter for making him like that, but Jupiter said it wasn't his fault. He had done the best he could for him, and, considering this was his only failing, he ought to be well content.

THE LION, JUPITER, AND THE ELEPHANT

The lion, however, wouldn't be comforted, and was so ashamed of his timidity that he wished he might die. In this state of mind he met the elephant and had a talk with him. He noticed that the great beast cocked up his ears all the time, as if he were listening for something, and he asked him why he did so. Just then a gnat came humming by, and the elephant said, "Do you see that wretched little buzzing insect? I'm terribly afraid of its getting into my ear. If it once gets in, I'm dead and done for." The lion's spirits rose at once when he heard this. "For," he said to himself, "if the elephant, huge as he is, is afraid of a gnat, I needn't be so much ashamed of being afraid of a cock, who is ten thousand times bigger than a gnat."

## 214. THE PIG AND THE SHEEP

A pig found his way into a meadow where a flock of sheep were grazing. The shepherd caught him, and was proceeding to carry him off to the butcher's when he set up a loud squealing and struggled to get free. The sheep rebuked him for making such a to-do, and said to him, "The shepherd catches us regularly and drags us off just like that, and we don't make any fuss." "No, I dare say not," replied the pig, "but my case and yours are altogether different. He only wants you for wool, but he wants me for bacon."

## 215. THE GARDENER AND HIS DOG

A gardener's dog fell into a deep well, from which his master used to draw water for the plants in his garden with a rope and a bucket. Failing to get the dog out by means of these, the gardener went down into the well himself in order to fetch him up. But the dog thought he had come to make sure of drowning him; so he bit his master as soon as he came within reach, and hurt him a good deal, with the result that he left the dog to his fate and climbed out of the well, remarking, "It serves me quite right for trying to save so determined a suicide."

## 216. THE RIVERS AND THE SEA

Once upon a time all the rivers combined to protest against the action of the sea in making their waters salt. "When we come to you," said they to the sea, "we are sweet and drink-able; but when once we have mingled with you, our waters become as briny and unpalatable as your own." The sea replied shortly, "Keep away from me, and you'll remain sweet."

## 217. THE LION IN LOVE

A lion fell deeply in love with the daughter of a cottager and wanted to marry her. But her father was unwilling to give her to so fearsome a husband, and yet didn't want to offend the lion; so he hit upon the following expedient. He went to the lion and said, "I think you will make a very good husband for my daughter; but I cannot consent to your union unless you let me draw your teeth and pare your nails, for my daughter is terribly afraid of them." The lion was so much in love that he readily agreed that this should be done. When once, however, he was thus disarmed, the cottager was afraid of him no longer, but drove him away with his club.

## 218. THE BEEKEEPER

A thief found his way into an apiary when the beekeeper was away, and stole all the honey. When the keeper returned and found the hives empty, he was very much upset and stood staring at them for some time. Before long the bees came back from gathering honey, and, finding their hives overturned and the keeper standing by, they made for him with their stings. At this he fell into a passion and cried, "You ungrateful scoundrels, you let the thief who stole my honey get off scot-free, and then you go and sting me who have always taken such care of you!"

When you hit back make sure you have got the right man.

## 219. THE WOLF AND THE HORSE

A wolf on his rambles came to a field of oats, but, not being able to eat them, he was passing on his way when a horse came along. "Look," said the wolf, "here's a fine field of oats. For your sake I have left it untouched, and I shall greatly enjoy the sound of your teeth munching the ripe grain." But the horse replied, "If wolves could eat oats, my fine friend, you would hardly have indulged your ears at the cost of your belly."

There is no virtue in giving to others what is useless to oneself.

THE WOLF AND THE HORSE

## 220 . THE BAT, THE BRAMBLE,
## AND THE SEAGULL

A bat, a bramble, and a seagull went into partnership and determined to go on a trading voyage together. The bat borrowed a sum of money for his venture; the bramble laid in a stock of clothes of various kinds; and the seagull took a quantity of lead. And so they set out. By and by a great storm came on, and their boat with all the cargo went to the bottom, but the three travelers managed to reach land. Ever since then the seagull flies to and fro over the sea, and every now and then dives below the surface looking for the lead he's lost; while the bat is so afraid of meeting his creditors that he hides away by day and only comes out at night to feed; and the bramble catches hold of the clothes of everyone who passes by, hoping some day to recognize and recover the lost garments.

**All men are more concerned to recover what they lose than to acquire what they lack.**

## 221 . THE DOG AND THE WOLF

A dog was lying in the sun before a farmyard gate when a wolf pounced upon him and was just going to eat him up. But he begged for his life and said, "You see how thin I am and what a wretched meal I should make you now. But if you will only wait a few days, my master is going to give a feast. All the rich scraps and pickings will fall to me, and I shall get nice and fat. Then will be the time for you to eat me." The wolf thought this was a very good plan and went away. Sometime afterwards he came to the farmyard again and found the dog lying out of reach on the stable roof. "Come down," he called, "and be eaten. You remember our agreement?" But the dog said coolly, "My friend, if ever you catch me lying down by the gate there again, don't you wait for any feast."

Once bitten, twice shy.

## 222. THE WASP AND THE SNAKE

A wasp settled on the head of a snake, and not only stung him several times, but clung obstinately to the head of his victim. Maddened with pain the snake tried every means he could think of to get rid of the creature, but without success. At last he became desperate, and crying, "Kill you I will, even at the cost of my own life," he laid his head with the wasp on it under the wheel of a passing wagon, and they both perished together.

## 223 · THE EAGLE AND THE BEETLE

An eagle was chasing a hare, which was running for dear life and was at her wits' end to know where to turn for help. Presently she espied a beetle and begged it to aid her. So when the eagle came up the beetle warned her not to touch the hare, which was under its protection. But the eagle never noticed the beetle because it was so small, seized the hare, and ate her up. The beetle never forgot this, and used to keep an eye on the eagle's nest, and whenever the eagle laid an egg it climbed up and rolled it out of the nest and broke it. At last the eagle got so worried over the loss of her eggs that she went up to Jupiter, who is the special protector of eagles, and begged him to give her a safe place to nest in; so he let her lay her eggs in his lap. But the beetle noticed this and made a ball of dirt the size of an eagle's egg, and flew up and deposited it in Jupiter's lap. When Jupiter saw the dirt, he stood up to shake it out of his robe, and, forgetting about the eggs, he shook them out too, and they were broken just as before. Ever since then, they say, eagles never lay their eggs at the season when beetles are about.

The weak will sometimes find ways to avenge an insult, even upon the strong.

## 224. THE FOWLER AND THE LARK

A fowler was setting his nets for little birds when a lark came up to him and asked him what he was doing. "I am engaged in founding a city," said he, and with that he withdrew to a short distance and concealed himself. The lark examined the nets with great curiosity, and presently, catching sight of the bait, hopped onto them in order to secure it, and became entangled in the meshes. The fowler then ran up quickly and captured her. "What a fool I was!" said she. "But at any rate, if that's the kind of city you are founding, it'll be a long time before you find fools enough to fill it."

## 225. THE FISHERMAN PIPING

A fisherman who could play the flute went down one day to the seashore with his nets and his flute; and, taking his stand on a projecting rock, began to play a tune, thinking that the music would bring the fish jumping out of the sea. He went on playing for some time, but not a fish appeared. So at last he threw down his flute and cast his net into the sea, and made a great haul of fish. When they were landed and he saw them leaping about on the shore, he cried, "You rascals! You wouldn't dance when I piped; but now I've stopped, you can do nothing else!"

## 226. THE WEASEL AND THE MAN

A man once caught a weasel which was always sneaking about the house, and was just going to drown it in a tub of water, when it begged hard for its life, and said to him, "Surely you haven't the heart to put me to death? Think how useful I have been in clearing your house of the mice and lizards which used to infest it, and show your gratitude by sparing my life." "You have not been altogether useless, I grant you," said the man. "But who killed the fowls? Who stole the meat? No, no! You do much more harm than good, and die you shall."

**THE FISHERMAN PIPING**

## 227. THE PLOWMAN, THE ASS, AND THE OX

A plowman yoked his ox and his ass together, and set to work to plow his field. It was a poor makeshift of a team, but it was the best he could do, as he had but a single ox. At the end of the day, when the beasts were loosed from the yoke, the ass said to the ox, "Well, we've had a hard day. Which of us is to carry the master home?" The ox looked surprised at the question. "Why," said he, "you, to be sure, as usual."

## 228. DEMADES AND HIS FABLE

Demades the orator was once speaking in the assembly at Athens. But the people were very inattentive to what he was saying, so he stopped and said, "Gentlemen, I should like to tell you one of Aesop's fables." This made everyone listen intently. Then Demades began, "Demeter, a swallow, and an eel were once traveling together, and came to a river without a bridge. The swallow flew over it, and the eel swam across." And then he stopped. "What happened to Demeter?" cried several people in the audience. "Demeter," he replied, "is very angry with you for listening to fables when you ought to be minding public business."

## 229 . THE MONKEY AND THE DOLPHIN

When people go on a voyage they often take with them lapdogs or monkeys as pets to while away the time. Thus it fell out that a man returning to Athens from the East had a pet monkey on board with him. As they neared the coast of Attica a great storm burst upon them, and the ship capsized. All on board were thrown into the water, and tried to save themselves by swimming, the monkey among the rest. A dolphin saw him, and, supposing him to be a man, took him on his back and began swimming towards the shore. When they got near the Piraeus, which is the port of Athens, the dolphin asked the monkey if he was an Athenian. The monkey replied that he was, and added that he came of a very distinguished family. "Then, of course, you know the Piraeus," continued the dolphin. The monkey thought he was referring to some high official or other, and replied, "Oh, yes, he's a very old friend of mine." At that, detecting his hypocrisy, the dolphin was so disgusted that he dived below the surface, and the unfortunate monkey was quickly drowned.

THE MONKEY AND THE DOLPHIN

## 230. THE CROW AND THE SNAKE

A hungry crow spied a snake lying asleep in a sunny spot, and, picking it up in his claws, he was carrying it off to a place where he could make a meal of it without being disturbed, when the snake reared its head and bit him. It was a poisonous snake, and the bite was fatal, and the dying crow said, "What a cruel fate is mine! I thought I had made a lucky find, and it has cost me my life!"

## 231. THE DOGS AND THE FOX

Some dogs once found a lion's skin, and were worrying it with their teeth. Just then a fox came by and said, "You think your-selves very brave, no doubt; but if that were a live lion, you'd find his claws a good deal sharper than your teeth."

## 232. THE NIGHTINGALE
## AND THE HAWK

A nightingale was sitting on a bough of an oak and singing, as her custom was. A hungry hawk presently spied her, and darting to the spot seized her in his talons. He was just about to tear her in pieces when she begged him to spare her life. "I'm not big enough," she pleaded, "to make you a good meal. You ought to seek your prey among the bigger birds." The hawk eyed her with some contempt. "You must think me very simple," said he, "if you suppose I am going to give up a certain prize on the chance of a better, of which I see at present no signs."

## 233. THE ROSE AND THE AMARANTH

A rose and an amaranth* blossomed side by side in a garden, and the amaranth said to her neighbor, "How I envy you your beauty and your sweet scent! No wonder you are such a universal favorite." But the rose replied with a shade of sadness in her voice, "Ah, my dear friend, I bloom but for a time. My petals soon wither and fall, and then I die. But your flowers never fade, even if they are cut; for they are everlasting."

---

*A mythical flower that never fades.

## 234. THE MAN, THE HORSE, THE OX, AND THE DOG

One winter's day during a severe storm a horse, an ox, and a dog came and begged for shelter in the house of a man. He readily admitted them, and, as they were cold and wet, he lit a fire for their comfort; and he put oats before the horse, and hay before the ox, while he fed the dog with the remains of his own dinner. When the storm abated, and they were about to depart, they determined to show their gratitude in the following way. They divided the life of man among them, and each endowed one part of it with the qualities which were peculiarly his own. The horse took youth, and hence young men are high-mettled and impatient of restraint; the ox took middle age, and accordingly men in middle life are steady and hard-working; while the dog took old age, which is the reason why old men are so often peevish and ill-tempered, and, like dogs, attached chiefly to those who look to their comfort, while they are disposed to snap at those who are unfamiliar or distasteful to them.

## 235. THE WOLVES, THE SHEEP,
## AND THE RAM

The wolves sent a deputation to the sheep with proposals for a lasting peace between them, on condition of their giving up the sheepdogs to instant death. The foolish sheep agreed to the terms; but an old ram, whose years had brought him wisdom, interfered and said, "How can we expect to live at peace with you? Why, even with the dogs at hand to protect us, we are never secure from your murderous attacks!"

## 236. THE SWAN

The swan is said to sing but once in its life—when it knows that it is about to die.* A certain man who had heard of the song of the swan one day saw one of these birds for sale in the market, and bought it and took it home with him. A few days later he had some friends to dinner, and produced the swan, and bade it sing for their entertainment; but the swan remained silent. In course of time, when it was growing old, it became aware of its approaching end and broke into a sweet, sad song. When its owner heard it, he said angrily, "If the creature only sings when it is about to die, what a fool I was that day I wanted to hear its song! I ought to have wrung its neck instead of merely inviting it to sing."

---

*This belief is the origin of the expression "swan song."

## 237. THE SNAKE AND JUPITER

A snake suffered a good deal from being constantly trodden upon by man and beast, owing partly to the length of his body and partly to his being unable to raise himself above the surface of the ground; so he went and complained to Jupiter about the risks to which he was exposed. But Jupiter had little sympathy for him. "I dare say," said he, "that if you had bitten the first that trod on you, the others would have taken more trouble to look where they put their feet."

## 238. THE WOLF AND HIS SHADOW

A wolf who was roaming about on the plain when the sun was getting low in the sky was much impressed by the size of his shadow, and said to himself, "I had no idea I was so big. Fancy my being afraid of a lion! Why, I, not he, ought to be king of the beasts." And, heedless of danger, he strutted about as if there could be no doubt at all about it. Just then a lion sprang upon him and began to devour him. "Alas," he cried, "had I not lost sight of the facts, I shouldn't have been ruined by my fancies."

## 239. THE PLOWMAN AND THE WOLF

A plowman loosed his oxen from the plow and led them away to the water to drink. While he was absent a half-starved wolf appeared on the scene, and went up to the plow and began chewing the leather straps attached to the yoke. As he gnawed away desperately in the hope of satisfying his craving for food, he somehow got entangled in the harness, and, taking fright, struggled to get free, tugging at the traces as if he would drag the plow along with him. Just then the plowman came back, and seeing what was happening, he cried, "Ah, you old rascal, I wish you would give up thieving for good and take to honest work instead."

## 240. MERCURY AND THE MAN BITTEN BY AN ANT

A man once saw a ship go down with all its crew, and commented severely on the injustice of the gods. "They care nothing for a man's character," said he, "but let the good and the bad go to their deaths together." There was an ant heap close by where he was standing, and, just as he spoke, he was bitten in the foot by an ant. Turning in a temper to the ant heap he stamped upon it and crushed hundreds of unoffending ants. Suddenly Mercury appeared, and belabored him with his staff, saying as he did so, "You villain, where's your nice sense of justice now?"

## 241. THE WILY LION

A lion watched a fat bull feeding in a meadow, and his mouth watered when he thought of the royal feast he would make, but he did not dare to attack him, for he was afraid of his sharp horns. Hunger, however, presently compelled him to do something; and as the use of force did not promise success, he determined to resort to artifice. Going up to the bull in friendly fashion, he said to him, "I cannot help saying how much I admire your magnificent figure. What a fine head! What powerful shoulders and thighs! But, my dear friend, what in the world makes you wear those ugly horns? You must find them as awkward as they are unsightly. Believe me, you would do much better without them." The bull was foolish enough to be persuaded by this flattery to have his horns cut off; and, having now lost his only means of defense, fell an easy prey to the lion.

## 242. THE PARROT AND THE CAT

A man once bought a parrot and gave it the run of his house. It reveled in its liberty, and presently flew up onto the mantelpiece and screamed away to its heart's content. The noise disturbed the cat, who was asleep on the hearthrug. Looking up at the intruder, she said, "Who may you be, and where have you come from?" The parrot replied, "Your master has just bought me and brought me home with him." "You impudent bird," said the cat, "how dare you, a newcomer, make a noise like that? Why, I was born here, and have lived here all my life, and yet, if I venture to mew, they throw things at me and chase me all over the place." "Look here, mistress," said the parrot; "you just hold your tongue. My voice they delight in, but yours—yours is a perfect nuisance."

## 243. THE STAG AND THE LION

A stag was chased by the hounds, and took refuge in a cave, where he hoped to be safe from his pursuers. Unfortunately the cave contained a lion, to whom he fell an easy prey. "Unhappy that I am," he cried, "I am saved from the power of the dogs only to fall into the clutches of a lion."

Out of the frying pan into the fire.

## 244 · THE IMPOSTER

A certain man fell ill, and, being in a very bad way, he made a vow that he would sacrifice a hundred oxen to the gods if they would grant him a return to health. Wishing to see how he would keep his vow, they caused him to recover in a short time. Now, he hadn't an ox in the world, so he made a hundred little oxen out of tallow and offered them up on an altar, at the same time saying, "Ye gods, I call you to witness that I have discharged my vow." The gods determined to be even with him, so they sent him a dream, in which he was bidden to go to the seashore and fetch a hundred crowns which he was to find there. Hastening in great excitement to the shore, he fell in with a band of robbers, who seized him and carried him off to sell as a slave. And when they sold him, a hundred crowns was the sum he fetched.

Do not promise more than you can perform.

## 245 · THE DOGS AND THE HIDES

Once upon a time a number of dogs, who were famished with hunger, saw some hides steeping in a river, but couldn't get at them because the water was too deep. So they put their heads together, and decided to drink away at the river till it was shallow enough for them to reach the hides. But long before that happened they burst themselves with drinking.

## 246. THE LION, THE FOX, AND THE ASS

A lion, a fox, and an ass went out hunting together. They had soon taken a large booty, which the lion requested the ass to divide between them. The ass divided it all into three equal parts, and modestly begged the others to take their choice; at which the lion, bursting with fury, sprang upon the ass and tore him to pieces. Then, glaring at the fox, he bade him make a fresh division. The fox gathered almost the whole in one great heap for the lion's share, leaving only the smallest possible morsel for himself. "My dear friend," said the lion, "how did you get the knack of it so well?" The fox replied, "Me? Oh, I took a lesson from the ass."

**Happy is he who learns from the misfortunes of others.**

## 247. THE FOWLER, THE PARTRIDGE,
## AND THE COCK

O ne day, as a fowler was sitting down to a scanty supper of herbs and bread, a friend dropped in unexpectedly. The larder was empty, so he went out and caught a tame partridge, which he kept as a decoy, and was about to wring her neck when she cried, "Surely you won't kill me? Why, what will you do without me next time you go fowling? How will you get the birds to come to your nets?" He let her go at this, and went to his hen house, where he had a plump young cock. When the cock saw what he was after, he too pleaded for his life, and said, "If you kill me, how will you know the time of night? And who will wake you up in the morning when it is time to get to work?" The fowler, however, replied, "You are useful for telling the time, I know; but, for all that, I can't send my friend supperless to bed." And therewith he caught him and wrung his neck.

## 248. THE GNAT AND THE LION

A gnat once went up to a lion and said, "I am not in the least afraid of you. I don't even allow that you are a match for me in strength. What does your strength amount to after all? That you can scratch with your claws and bite with your teeth— just like a woman in a temper—and nothing more. But I'm stronger than you. If you don't believe it, let us fight and see." So saying, the gnat sounded his horn, and darted in and bit the lion on the nose. When the lion felt the sting, in his haste to crush him, he scratched his nose badly and made it bleed, but failed altogether to hurt the

**THE GNAT AND THE LION**

gnat, which buzzed off in triumph, elated by its victory. Presently, however, it got entangled in a spider's web and was caught and eaten by the spider, thus falling prey to an insignificant insect after having triumphed over the king of the beasts.

## 249. THE FARMER AND HIS DOGS

A farmer was snowed up in his farmstead by a severe storm and was unable to go out and procure provisions for himself and his family. So he first killed his sheep and used them for food. Then, as the storm still continued, he killed his goats. And, last of all, as the weather showed no signs of improving, he was compelled to kill his oxen and eat them. When his dogs saw the various animals being killed and eaten in turn, they said to one another, "We had better get out of this, or we shall be the next to go!"

## 250. THE EAGLE AND THE FOX

An eagle and a fox became great friends and determined to live near one another. They thought that the more they saw of each other the better friends they would be. So the eagle built a nest at the top of a high tree, while the fox settled in a thicket at the foot of it and produced a litter of cubs. One day the fox went out foraging for food, and the eagle, who also wanted food for her young, flew down into the thicket, caught up the fox's cubs, and carried them up into the tree for a meal for herself and her family.

When the fox came back and found out what had happened, she was not so much sorry for the loss of her cubs as furious because she couldn't get at the eagle and pay her back for her treachery. So she sat down not far off and cursed her. But it wasn't long before she had her revenge. Some villagers happened to be sacrificing a goat on a neighboring altar, and the eagle flew down and carried off a piece of burning flesh to her nest. There was a strong wind blowing, and the nest caught fire, with the result that her fledglings fell half roasted to the ground. Then the fox ran to the spot and devoured them in full sight of the eagle.

**False faith may escape human punishment, but cannot escape the divine.**

## 251. THE BUTCHER AND HIS CUSTOMERS

Two men were buying meat at a butcher's stall in the market-place, and, while the butcher's back was turned for a moment, one of them snatched up a joint and hastily thrust it under the other's cloak, where it could not be seen. When the butcher turned round, he missed the meat at once, and charged them with having stolen it; but the one who had taken it said he didn't have it, and the one who had it said he hadn't taken it. The butcher felt sure they were deceiving him, but he only said, "You may cheat me with your lying, but you can't cheat the gods, and they won't let you off so lightly."

**Prevarication often amounts to perjury.**

## 252. HERCULES AND MINERVA

Hercules was once traveling along a narrow road when he saw lying on the ground in front of him what appeared to be an apple, and as he passed he stamped upon it with his heel. To his astonishment, instead of being crushed it doubled in size; and, on his attacking it again and smiting it with his club, it swelled up to an enormous size and blocked up the whole road. Upon this he dropped his club and stood looking at it in amazement. Just then Minerva appeared and said to him, "Leave it alone, my friend. That which you see before you is the Apple of Discord.* If you do not meddle with it, it remains small as it was at first, but if you resort to violence it swells into the thing you see."

## 253. THE FOX WHO SERVED A LION

A lion had a fox to attend on him, and whenever they went hunting the fox found the prey, and the lion fell upon it and killed it, and then they divided it between them in certain proportions. But the lion always got a very large share and the fox a very small one, which didn't please the latter at all; so he determined to set up on his own account. He began by trying to steal a

---

*Reminiscent of Pandora's box in Greek mythology.

lamb from a flock of sheep. But the shepherd saw him and set his dogs on him. The hunter was now the hunted, and was very soon caught and dispatched by the dogs.

**Better servitude with safety than freedom with danger.**

## 254. THE QUACK DOCTOR

A certain man fell sick and took to his bed. He consulted a number of doctors from time to time, and they all, with one exception, told him that his life was in no immediate danger, but that his illness would probably last a considerable time. The one who took a different view of his case, who was also the last to be consulted, bade him prepare for the worst. "You have not twenty-four hours to live," said he, "and I fear I can do nothing." As it turned out, however, he was quite wrong; for at the end of a few days the sick man quitted his bed and took a walk abroad, looking, it is true, as pale as a ghost. In the course of his walk he met the doctor who had prophesied his death. "Dear me," said the latter. "How do you do? You are fresh from the other world, no doubt. Pray, how are our departed friends getting on there?" "Most comfortably," replied the other, "for they have drunk the water of oblivion and have forgotten all the troubles of life. By the way, just before I left, the authorities were making arrangements to prosecute all the doctors, because they won't let sick men die in the course of nature, but use their arts to keep them alive. They were going to charge you along with the rest, till I assured them that you were no doctor, but a mere impostor."

## 255 · THE LION, THE WOLF,
## AND THE FOX

A lion, infirm with age, lay sick in his den, and all the beasts of the forest came to inquire after his health, with the exception of the fox. The wolf thought this was a good opportunity for paying off old scores against the fox, so he called the attention of the lion to his absence, and said, "You see, sire, that we have all come to see how you are, except the fox, who hasn't come near you, and doesn't care whether you are well or ill." Just then the fox came in and heard the last words of the wolf. The lion roared at him in deep displeasure, but he begged to be allowed to explain his absence and said, "Not one of them cares for you so much as I, sire, for all the time I have been going round to the doctors and trying to find a cure for your illness." "And may I ask if you have found one?" said the lion. "I have, sire," said the fox, "and it is this. You must flay a wolf and wrap yourself in his skin while it is still warm." The lion accordingly turned to the wolf and struck him dead with one blow of his paw, in order to try the fox's prescription; but the fox laughed and said to himself, "That's what comes of stirring up ill will."

## 256. HERCULES AND PLUTUS

When Hercules was received among the gods and was entertained at a banquet by Jupiter, he responded courteously to the greetings of all with the exception of Plutus, the god of wealth. When Plutus approached him, he cast his eyes upon the ground, and turned away and pretended not to see him. Jupiter was surprised at this conduct on his part, and asked why, after having been so cordial with all the other gods, he had behaved like that to Plutus. "Sire," said Hercules, "I do not like Plutus, and I will tell you why. When we were on earth together I always noticed that he was to be found in the company of scoundrels."

## 257 · THE FOX AND THE LEOPARD

A fox and a leopard were disputing about their looks, and each claimed to be the more handsome of the two. The leopard said, "Look at my smart coat. You have nothing to match that." But the fox replied, "Your coat may be smart, but my wits are smarter still."

## 258 · THE FOX AND THE HEDGEHOG

A fox, in swimming across a rapid river, was swept away by the current and carried a long way downstream in spite of his struggles, until at last, bruised and exhausted, he managed to scramble onto dry ground from a backwater. As he lay there unable to move, a swarm of horseflies settled on him and sucked his blood undisturbed, for he was too weak even to shake them off. A hedgehog saw him, and asked if he should brush away the flies that were tormenting him; but the fox replied, "Oh, please, no, not on any account, for these flies have sucked their fill and are taking very little from me now. But if you drive them off, another swarm of hungry ones will come and suck all the blood I have left, and leave me without a drop in my veins."

## 259. THE CROW AND THE RAVEN

A crow became very jealous of a raven, because the latter was regarded by men as a bird of omen which foretold the future, and was accordingly held in great respect by them. She was very anxious to get the same sort of reputation herself; and, one day, seeing some travelers approaching, she flew onto a branch of a tree at the roadside and cawed as loud as she could. The travelers were in some dismay at the sound, for they feared it might be a bad omen, till one of them, spying the crow, said to his companions, "It's all right, my friends, we can go on without fear, for it's only a crow and that means nothing."

**Those who pretend to be something they are not, only make themselves ridiculous.**

## 260. THE WITCH

A witch professed to be able to avert the anger of the gods by means of charms, of which she alone possessed the secret; and she drove a brisk trade, and made a fat livelihood out of it. But certain persons accused her of black magic and carried her before the judges, and demanded that she should be put to death for dealings with the devil. She was found guilty and condemned to death; and one of the judges said to her as she was leaving the dock, "You say you can avert the anger of the gods. How comes it, then, that you have failed to disarm the enmity of men?"

## 261. THE OLD MAN AND DEATH

An old man cut himself a bundle of sticks in a wood and started to carry them home. He had a long way to go, and was tired out before he had got much more than halfway. Casting his burden on the ground, he called upon Death to come and release him from his life of toil. The words were scarcely out of his mouth when, much to his dismay, Death stood before him and professed his readiness to serve him. He was almost frightened out of his wits, but he had enough presence of mind to stammer out, "Good sir, if you'd be so kind, pray help me up with my burden again."

THE MISER

## 262. THE MISER

A miser sold everything he had, and melted down his hoard of gold into a single lump, which he buried secretly in a field. Every day he went to look at it, and would sometimes spend long hours gloating over his treasure. One of his men noticed his frequent visits to the spot, and one day watched him and discovered his secret. Waiting his opportunity, he went one night and dug up the gold and stole it. Next day the miser visited the place as usual, and, finding his treasure gone, fell to tearing his hair and groaning over his loss. In this condition he was seen by one of his neighbors, who asked him what his trouble was. The miser told him of his misfortune; but the other replied, "Don't take it so much to heart, my friend; put a brick into the hole, and take a look at it every day. You won't be any worse off than before, for even when you had your gold it was of no earthly use to you."

## 263. THE FOXES AND THE RIVER

A number of foxes assembled on the bank of a river and wanted to drink. But the current was so strong and the water looked so deep and dangerous that they didn't dare to do so, but stood near the edge encouraging one another not to be afraid. At last one of them, to shame the rest and show how brave he was, said, "I am not a bit frightened! See, I'll step right into the water!" He had no sooner done so than the current swept him off his feet. When the others saw him being carried downstream they cried,

"Don't go and leave us! Come back and show us where we too can drink with safety." But he replied, "I'm afraid I can't yet. I want to go to the seaside, and this current will take me there nicely. When I come back I'll show you with pleasure."

## 264. THE HORSE AND THE STAG

There was once a horse who used to graze in a meadow which he had all to himself. But one day a stag came into the meadow, and said he had as good a right to feed there as the horse, and moreover chose all the best places for himself. The horse, wishing to be revenged upon his unwelcome visitor, went to a man and asked if he would help him to turn out the stag. "Yes," said the man, "I will by all means; but I can only do so if you let me put a bridle in your mouth and mount on your back." The horse agreed to this, and the two together very soon turned the stag out of the pasture. But when that was done, the horse found to his dismay that in the man he had got a master for good.

## 265. THE FOX AND THE BRAMBLE

In making his way through a hedge a fox missed his footing and caught at a bramble to save himself from falling. Naturally, he got badly scratched, and in disgust he cried to the bramble, "It was your help I wanted, and see how you have treated me! I'd sooner have fallen outright." The bramble, interrupting him, replied, "You must have lost your wits, my friend, to catch at me, who am myself always catching at others."

## 266. THE FOX AND THE SNAKE

A snake, in crossing a river, was carried away by the current, but managed to wriggle onto a bundle of thorns which was floating by, and was thus carried at a great rate downstream. A fox caught sight of it from the bank as it went whirling along, and called out, "Gad! The passenger fits the ship!"

## 267. THE LION, THE FOX, AND THE STAG

A lion lay sick in his den, unable to provide himself with food. So he said to his friend the fox, who came to ask how he did, "My good friend, I wish you would go to yonder wood and beguile the big stag who lives there to come to my den. I have a fancy to make my dinner off a stag's heart and brains." The fox went to the wood and found the stag and said to him, "My dear sir, you're in luck. You know the lion, our king. Well, he's at the point of death, and has appointed you his successor to rule over the beasts. I hope you won't forget that I was the first to bring you the good news. And now I must be going back to him, and, if you take my advice, you'll come too and be with him at the last."

The stag was highly flattered, and followed the fox to the lion's den, suspecting nothing. No sooner had he got inside than the lion sprang upon him, but he misjudged his spring, and the stag got away with only his ears torn and returned as fast as he could to the shelter of the wood. The fox was much mortified, and the lion, too, was dreadfully disappointed, for he was getting very hungry in spite of his illness. So he begged the fox to have another try at coaxing the stag to his den. "It'll be almost impossible this time," said the fox, "but I'll try." And off he went to the wood a second time, and found the stag resting and trying to recover from his fright.

As soon as he saw the fox he cried, "You scoundrel, what do you mean by trying to lure me to my death like that? Take yourself off, or I'll do you to death with my horns." But the fox was entirely shameless. "What a coward you were," said he. "Surely you didn't think the lion meant any harm? Why, he was only going to whisper some royal secrets into your ear when you went off like a scared rabbit. You have rather disgusted him, and I'm not sure he won't make the wolf king instead, unless you come back at once and show you've got some spirit. I promise you he won't hurt you, and I will be your faithful servant."

The stag was foolish enough to be persuaded to return, and this time the lion made no mistake, but overpowered him, and feasted right royally upon his carcass. The fox, meanwhile, watched his chance and, when the lion wasn't looking, filched away the brains* to reward him for his trouble. Presently the lion began searching for them, of course without success; and the fox, who was watching him, said, "I don't think it's much use your looking for the brains. A creature who twice walked into a lion's den can't have had any."

---

*In the original Greek text it was the heart that was stolen, which in antiquity was believed to be the seat of intelligence.

## 268. THE MAN WHO LOST HIS SPADE

A man was engaged in digging over his vineyard, and one day on coming to work he missed his spade. Thinking it may have been stolen by one of his labourers, he questioned them closely, but they one and all denied any knowledge of it. He was not convinced by their denials, and insisted that they should all go to the town and take oath in a temple that they were not guilty of the theft. This was because he had no great opinion of the simple country deities, but thought that the thief would not pass undetected by the shrewder gods of the town. When they got inside the gates the first thing they heard was the town crier proclaiming a reward for information about a thief who had stolen something from the city temple. "Well," said the man to himself, "it strikes me I had better go back home again. If these town gods can't detect the thieves who steal from their own temples, it's scarcely likely they can tell me who stole my spade."

## 269. THE PARTRIDGE AND THE FOWLER

A fowler caught a partridge in his nets, and was just about to wring its neck when it made a piteous appeal to him to spare its life and said, "Do not kill me, but let me live and I will repay you for your kindness by decoying other partridges into your nets." "No," said the fowler, "I will not spare you. I was going to kill you anyhow, and after that treacherous speech you thoroughly deserve your fate."

## 270.  THE RUNAWAY SLAVE

A slave, being discontented with his lot, ran away from his master. He was soon missed by the latter, who lost no time in mounting his horse and setting out in pursuit of the fugitive. He presently came up with him, and the slave, in the hope of avoiding capture, slipped into a treadmill* and hid himself there. "Aha," said his master, "that's the very place for you, my man!"

## 271.  THE HUNTER AND THE WOODMAN

A hunter was searching in the forest for the tracks of a lion, and, catching sight presently of a woodman engaged in felling a tree, he went up to him and asked him if he had noticed a lion's footprints anywhere about, or if he knew where his den was. The woodman answered, "If you will come with me, I will show you the lion himself." The hunter turned pale with fear, and his teeth chattered as he replied, "Oh, I'm not looking for the lion, thanks, but only for his tracks."

---

*Where the recaptured slave will be forced to labor.

## 272. THE SERPENT AND THE EAGLE

An eagle swooped down upon a serpent and seized it in his talons with the intention of carrying it off and devouring it. But the serpent was too quick for him and had its coils round him in a moment; and then there ensued a life–and–death struggle between the two. A countryman, who was a witness of the encounter, came to the assistance of the eagle, and succeeded in freeing him from the serpent and enabling him to escape. In revenge the serpent spat some of his poison into the man's drinking horn. Heated with his exertions, the man was about to slake his thirst with a draft from the horn, when the eagle knocked it out of his hand and spilled its contents upon the ground.

**One good turn deserves another.**

## 273 · THE ROGUE AND THE ORACLE

A rogue laid a wager that he would prove the Oracle at Delphi to be untrustworthy by procuring from it a false reply to an inquiry by himself. So he went to the temple on the appointed day with a small bird in his hand, which he concealed under the folds of his cloak, and asked whether what he held in his hand were alive or dead. If the Oracle said "dead," he meant to produce the bird alive. If the reply was "alive," he intended to wring its neck and show it to be dead. But the Oracle was one too many for him, for the answer he got was this: "Stranger, whether the thing that you hold in your hand be alive or dead is a matter that depends entirely on your own will."

## 274. THE HORSE AND THE ASS

A horse, proud of his fine harness, met an ass on the high road. As the ass with his heavy burden moved slowly out of the way to let him pass, the horse cried out impatiently that he could hardly resist kicking him to make him move faster. The ass held his peace, but did not forget the other's insolence. Not long afterwards the horse became broken-winded and was sold by his owner to a farmer. One day, as he was drawing a dung cart, he met the ass again, who in turn derided him and said, "Aha! You never thought to come to this, did you, you who were so proud! Where are all your gay trappings now?"

## 275. THE DOG CHASING A WOLF

A dog was chasing a wolf, and as he ran he thought what a fine fellow he was, and what strong legs he had, and how quickly they covered the ground. "Now, there's this wolf," he said to himself. "What a poor creature he is. He's no match for me, and he knows it and so he runs away." But the wolf looked round just then and said, "Don't you imagine I'm running away from you, my friend. It's your master I'm afraid of."

## 276. GRIEF AND HIS DUE

When Jupiter was assigning the various gods their privileges, it so happened that Grief was not present with the rest; but when all had received their share, he too entered and claimed his due. Jupiter was at a loss to know what to do, for there was nothing left for him. However, at last he decided that to him should belong the tears that are shed for the dead. Thus it is the same with Grief as it is with the other gods. The more devoutly men render to him his due, the more lavish is he of that which he has to bestow. It is not well, therefore, to mourn long for the departed, else Grief, whose sole pleasure is in such mourning, will be quick to send fresh cause for tears.

## 277. THE HAWK, THE KITE,
## AND THE PIGEONS

The pigeons in a certain dovecote were persecuted by a kite,* who every now and then swooped down and carried off one of their number. So they invited a hawk into the dovecote to defend them against their enemy. But they soon repented of their folly; for the hawk killed more of them in a day than the kite had done in a year.

## 278. THE WOMAN AND THE FARMER

A woman who had lately lost her husband used to go every day to his grave and lament her loss. A farmer, who was engaged in plowing not far from the spot, set eyes upon the woman and desired to have her for his wife. So he left his plow and came and sat by her side and began to shed tears himself. She asked him why he wept; and he replied, "I have lately lost my wife, who was very dear to me, and tears ease my grief." "And I," said she, "have lost my husband." And so for a while they mourned in silence. Then he said, "Since you and I are in like case, shall we not do well to marry and live together? I shall take the place of your dead husband, and you, that of my dead wife." The woman consented to the plan, which indeed seemed reasonable enough, and they dried their

---

*A small hawk.

tears. Meanwhile, a thief had come, and stolen the oxen which the farmer had left with his plow. On discovering the theft, he beat his breast and loudly bewailed his loss. When the woman heard his cries, she came and said, "Why, are you weeping still?" To which he replied, "Yes, and I mean it this time."

## 279. PROMETHEUS AND THE MAKING OF MAN

At the bidding of Jupiter, Prometheus set about the creation of man and the other animals. Jupiter, seeing that mankind, the only rational creatures, were far outnumbered by the irrational beasts, bade him redress the balance by turning some of the latter into men. Prometheus did as he was bidden, and this is the reason why some people have the forms of men but the souls of beasts.

## 280. THE SWALLOW AND THE CROW

A swallow was once boasting to a crow about her birth. "I was once a princess," said she, "the daughter of a king of Athens, but my husband used me cruelly, and cut out my tongue for a slight fault. Then, to protect me from further injury, I was turned by Juno into a bird." "You chatter quite enough as it is," said the crow. "What you would have been like if you hadn't lost your tongue, I can't think."

## 281. THE HUNTER AND
## THE HORSEMAN

A hunter went out after game, and succeeded in catching a hare, which he was carrying home with him when he met a man on horseback, who said to him, "You have had some sport I see, sir," and offered to buy it. The hunter readily agreed; but the horseman had no sooner got the hare in his hands than he set spurs to his horse and went off at full gallop. The hunter ran after him for some little distance. But it soon dawned upon him that he had been tricked, and he gave up trying to overtake the horseman, and, to save his face, called after him as loud as he could, "All right, sir, all right. Take your hare. It was meant all along as a present."

## 282. THE GOATHERD AND
## THE WILD GOATS

A goatherd was tending his goats out at pasture when he saw a number of wild goats approach and mingle with his flock. At the end of the day he drove them home and put them all into the pen together. Next day the weather was so bad that he could not take them out as usual, so he kept them at home in the pen and fed them there. He only gave his own goats enough food to keep them from starving, but he gave the wild goats as much as they could eat and more; for he was very anxious for them to stay, and he thought that if he fed them well they wouldn't want to leave him.

When the weather improved he took them all out to pasture again, but no sooner had they got near the hills than the wild goats broke away from the flock and scampered off. The goatherd was very much disgusted at this, and roundly abused them for their ingratitude. "Rascals!" he cried. "To run away like that after the way I've treated you!" Hearing this, one of them turned round and said, "Oh, yes, you treated us all right—too well, in fact. It was just that that put us on our guard. If you treat newcomers like ourselves so much better than your own flock, it's more than likely that, if another lot of strange goats joined yours, we should then be neglected in favor of the last comers."

## 283. THE NIGHTINGALE
## AND THE SWALLOW

A swallow, conversing with a nightingale, advised her to quit the leafy coverts where she made her home, and to come and live with men, like herself, and nest under the shelter of their roofs. But the nightingale replied, "Time was when I too, like yourself, lived among men. But the memory of the cruel wrongs I then suffered makes them hateful to me, and never again will I approach their dwellings."

**The scene of past sufferings revives painful memories.**

## 284. THE TRAVELER AND FORTUNE

A traveler, exhausted with fatigue after a long journey, sank down at the very brink of a deep well and presently fell asleep. He was within an ace of falling in, when Lady Fortune appeared to him and touched him on the shoulder, cautioning him to move farther away. "Wake up, good sir, I pray you," she said. "Had you fallen into the well, the blame would have been thrown not on your own folly but on me, Fortune."

**Aesop.** For an account of Aesop's legendary life, see the early pages of this volume and the Introduction.

**Apollo.** One of the most highly revered and respected of all the Greek gods, he presided over many aspects of life and culture, including law, religion, poetry, and music. He is often depicted playing the lyre. The most important center for Apollo worship in ancient Greece was at Delphi, where he often revealed the future through his oracle.

**Athens.** The principal city of Attica, it was the center of ancient Greek civilization.

**Attica.** In this ancient district in east central Greece, Athens was the principal city.

**Death.** Cultural anthropologists have long noted that primitive peoples rarely have the ability to accept death as a natural and inevitable phenomenon. Thus the origin of death is described in myths from around the world, and personifications of death (for example, the Grim Reaper or the Angel of Death) are part of folk beliefs in many cultures. The character named Death in fable no. 261 is such a personification, a supernatural being who causes humans to die. However, his verdicts apparently are not necessarily final. This story, like many other folktales from around the world, shows an intended victim bargaining with his would-be captor with at least the hope of reprieve, but given the often cynical tone of Aesop's fables, most readers will not give him good chances of success.

**Delphi.** This city in ancient Greece was located on the slopes of Mount Parnassus. An important cultural center, Delphi was especially renowned as the location of the Oracle of Apollo.

**Demades.** An Athenian diplomat famous for his oratory skills, Demades lived between about 380 B.C. and 319 B.C.

**Demeter.** The name of this Greek goddess of agriculture can mean either "grain mother" or "mother earth." Her Roman equivalent was Ceres.

**Earth, Goddess of the.** The ancient Greeks worshiped a female personification of the earth whom they named Gaea. This Mother Earth figure is sometimes depicted as an adversary of Zeus, leading to the conjecture that in prehistoric times her cult was replaced by a religion centered around Zeus.

**Fortune, Lady.** According to ancient Greek belief, human destiny (especially the length of one's life and one's allotment of happiness and misery) was determined by three goddesses called fates. The Lady Fortune in fable no. 284 (also the Fortune of fable no. 56) may be one of these fates, or possibly an embodiment of all three. In Roman mythology the roles of the Greek fates were played by the Parcae (singular, Parca), whose names were Nona, Decuma, and Morta.

**Gods and mortals.** The morality of Aesop's fables is secular and pragmatic, and is rarely tied to religion, although the gods themselves, as well as other mythical beings, often play roles. These stories are, for the most part, of Greek origin, but they have come to us through the intermediacy of the Romans, so in the fables mythical beings are usually identified by their Roman names.

**Grief.** Although Grief is identified as a god in fable no. 276, no such specific deity is mentioned in most descriptions of Greek and Roman religion. This Aesopic fable is personifying the concept of grief into a supernatural being in much the same way that the concept of death is often personified.

**Hercules.** This is the Roman name of Heracles, the most famous of all Greek legendary heroes. Enormously strong and fiercely brave, Hercules was nevertheless forced into servitude and was able to free himself only by performing twelve labors. These tasks consisted for the most part in subduing terrifying mythical monsters, but one of them was the humiliating chore of cleaning dung from the stables of King Augeas, which he succeeded in doing by diverting two rivers and flooding the stables.

**Hymettus.** (Imittós), In ancient times this mountain in Greece, southeast of Athens, was famous for its aromatic herbs and for the unusually flavored honey that they produced.

**Juno.** She was the female counterpart of Jupiter (Jove), the principal deity in Roman religion. Her Greek counterpart was Hera.

**Jupiter.** (Also known as Jove), Jupiter was the Sky-God and the principal deity in pre-Christian Roman religion. In most Latin-rooted languages his name is still attached to the fifth day of the week—for example, *Jovis dies* (Latin), *jeudi* (French), and *jueves* (Spanish). Jupiter's counterpart in Greek mythology was Zeus.

**Mercury.** The Roman god of merchants, Mercury is identified with the Greek deity Hermes, who, according to Homer, served as the gods' messenger. Because of this association, Mercury is often portrayed with a winged helmet or winged sandals. In most Latin-rooted languages his name is still attached to the fourth day of the week—for example, *Mercurii dies* (Latin), *mercredi* (French), and *miércoles* (Spanish).

**Minerva.** In Roman mythology, Minerva presided over the arts and crafts and their associated skills. Because these skills could also be used in battle, she also came to be recognized as a goddess of warfare, making her a counterpart to the Greek goddess Athena.

**Olympus.** A snow-capped peak of nearly 10,000 feet in northern Greece, Mount Olympus was held to be the home of the gods by the ancient Greeks.

**Oracle at Delphi.** The word "oracle" can designate either an intermediary (such as a priestess) who communicates messages from a deity, the place (for example, a temple) where these revelations are received, or the divine message itself. The most important divination center in ancient Greece was the Oracle of Apollo at Delphi, a city located on the slopes of Mount Parnassus.

**Plutus.** The Greek god of wealth, especially agricultural abundance, Plutus is often depicted in art as a boy with a cornucopia.

**Prometheus.** The most famous of the Titans, a race of giants that inhabited the earth before humans were created, Prometheus is said to have formed the first humans out of clay and was their principal supporter before the gods. He is best remembered for attempting to benefit humankind by stealing fire from heaven for their use.

**Rhodes.** On this easternmost of the Greek islands, just off the coast of Turkey, the capital city is also named Rhodes.

**Satyr.** A creature in Greek mythology, a satyr is usually depicted as half man and half horse (or goat). Associated with Dionysus, god of wine and revelry, satyrs are marked by uncouth, licentious behavior. The most famous satyr was the Greek fertility deity Pan, often depicted playing shepherd's pipes and immortalized in such words as "panic" and "pandemonium." The Roman counterparts of satyrs were the fauns.

**Thebes.** According to tradition, King Oedipus held court at Thebes, one of the principal cities of ancient Greece. It is the setting of many classical tragedies by Aeschylus and Sophocles. The Greek Thebes should not be confused with the ancient Egyptian city of the same name.

**Theseus.** A legendary Greek hero and King of Athens, Theseus greatly admired the feats of Heracles (Hercules) and attempted to make a similar name for himself by seeking out contests with a variety of powerful opponents, including the Minotaur, a fabulous beast with the head of a bull and a human's body. Theseus, identified as the duke of Athens, is featured in two of Shakespeare's plays, *A Midsummer Night's Dream* and *Two Noble Kinsmen*.

**Venus.** An ancient Roman deity for agriculture, Venus also came to be associated with the Greek goddess of sexuality and love, Aphrodite, at a very early time. In most Latin-rooted languages Venus's name is still attached to the sixth day of the week—for example, *Veneris dies* (Latin), *vendredi* (French), and *viernes* (Spanish). Venus's male counterpart was her own son (fathered by Mercury) Cupid, called Amor by Roman poets. Cupid's Greek counterpart was Eros, the god of love.

# APPENDIX

*Aesopic Fables and Their Aarne-Thompson Type Numbers*

The Fox and the Grapes (no. 1), type 59
The Goose that Laid the Golden Eggs (no. 2), type 776
The Cat and the Mice (no. 3), type 113*
The Mice in Council (no. 6), type 110
The Fox and the Crow (no. 9), type 57
The Wolf and the Lamb (no. 11), type 111A
Mercury and the Woodman (no. 17), type 729
The Lion and the Mouse (no. 19), type 75
The Crow and the Pitcher (no. 20), type 232D*
The North Wind and the Sun (no. 22), type 298
The Mistress and Her Servants (no. 23), type 1566A*
The Hares and the Frogs (no. 25), type 70
The Fox and the Stork (no. 26), type 60
The Wolf in Sheep's Clothing (no. 27), type 123B
The Stag in the Ox-Stall (no. 28), type 162
The Milkmaid and Her Pail (no. 29), type 1430
The Ass and the Lapdog (no. 32), type 214
The Gnat and the Bull (no. 36), type 281
The Bear and the Travelers (no. 37), type 179
The Slave and the Lion (no. 38), type 156
The Oak and the Reeds (no. 41), type 298C*
The Ass and His Burdens (no. 45), type 211
The Shepherd's Boy and the Wolf (no. 46), type 1333
The Fox and the Goat (no. 47), type 31
The Fisherman and the Sprat (no. 48), type 122F
The Crab and His Mother (no. 50), type 276
The Farmer and His Sons (no. 52), type 910E
Jupiter and the Monkey (no. 57), type 247

Father and Sons (no. 58), type 910F

The Owl and the Birds (no. 60), type 233C

The Ass in the Lion's Skin (no. 61), type 214B

The Old Lion (no. 63), type 50A

The Swollen Fox (no. 66), type 41*

The Mouse, the Frog, and the Hawk (no. 67), type 278

The Jackdaw and the Pigeons (no. 70), type 244

The Boy and the Filberts (no. 75), type 68A

The Frogs Asking for a King (no. 76), type 277

The Tortoise and the Eagle (no. 81), type 225

The Kid on the Housetop (no. 82), type 127A*

The Fox without a Tail (no. 83), type 64

The Vain Jackdaw (no. 84), type 244

The Stag at the Pool (no. 93), type 77

The Dog and His Reflection (no. 94), type 34A

The Ox and the Frog (no. 100), type 277A

The Man and the Image (no. 101), type 1643

The Two Soldiers and the Robber (no. 106), similar to type 179

The Lion and the Wild Ass (no. 107), type 51

The Man and the Satyr (no. 108), type 1342

The Wolf, the Mother, and Her Child (no. 112), type 75*

The Cat and the Cock (no. 116), type 111A

The Hare and the Tortoise (no. 117), type 275A

The Lion and the Three Bulls (no. 122), type 119B*

The Lark and the Farmer (no. 128), type 93

The Wolf and the Crane (no. 134), type 76

The Town Mouse and the Country Mouse (no. 141), type 112

Venus and the Cat (no. 147), similar to type 402

The Grasshopper and the Ants (no. 156), type 280A

The Cobbler Turned Doctor (no. 159), similar to type 1641

The Belly and the Members (no. 161), type 293

The Bald Man and the Fly (no. 162), similar to type 1586

The Ass and the Wolf (no. 163), type 122J

The Birds, the Beasts, and the Bat (no. 168), type 222A

The Man and His Two Mistresses (no. 169), type 1215A

The Miller, His Son, and Their Ass (no. 172), type 1215

The Archer and the Lion (no. 175), similar to type 157

The Ass and the Mule (no. 178), type 207B

The Laborer and the Snake (no. 188), type 285D
The Bat, the Bramble, and the Seagull (no. 220), type 289
The Dog and the Wolf (no. 221), type 122F
The Nightingale and the Hawk (no. 232), similar to type 122E
The Man, the Horse, the Ox, and the Dog (no. 234), type 173
The Lion, the Fox, and the Ass (no. 246), type 51
The Gnat and the Lion (no. 248), type 281A*
The Lion, the Wolf, and the Fox (no. 255), type 50
The Old Man and Death (no. 261), type 845
The Miser (no. 262), type 1305B
The Foxes and the River (no. 263), type 67
The Lion, the Fox, and the Stag (no. 267), type 52
The Serpent and the Eagle (no. 272), similar to type 178
The Woman and the Farmer (no. 278), similar to type 1510

All animals are equal, but some animals are more equal than others.
—George Orwell, *Animal Farm*

Aesop (or the group of ancient storytellers we call Aesop) is famed for his mastery of the moral fable, or apologue, a distant cousin of the apology. "Apologue" comes from the Greek word meaning "defense," and the apology as literary form is exactly that: a defense of the writer's point of view. Aesop created apologues to inform his audience's morality and point a critical finger at the authorities, yet his oblique approach saved him from censure. Over the centuries the form has been employed by figures as diverse as Socrates and Sir Philip Sidney.

### *Orwell's* Animal Farm

Perhaps the twentieth century's finest example is George Orwell's *Animal Farm* (1945) political fable, which predicts the author's masterpiece *Nineteen Eighty-Four* (1949), Orwell makes use of a biting wit comparable to that of the eighteenth-century satirist Jonathan Swift. Assigning farm animals the roles of Stalin, Trotsky, and the common man, Orwell writes a pessimistic allegory about the tyranny of world leaders and the foibles of the Bolshevik and every other revolution. The anti-utopian *Animal Farm* is prized for its simple, direct style and profound moral stance. In his review of the novel in the *New York Times Book Review*, Arthur M. Schlesinger, Jr., wrote, "The story should be read in particular by liberals who cannot understand how Soviet performance has fallen so far behind Communist professions. 'Animal Farm' is a wise, compassionate and illuminated fable for our times."

## Aesop in the World's Lexicon

The fable as a form predates Aesop. Originating as long as 4,000 years ago, fables have enjoyed immense popularity throughout recorded time, in part because many of the proverbs and other expressions they contain are eminently quotable—so much so that these simple truths have been absorbed into the common wisdom of our species.

Aesop proved especially adept at creating situations and wordings that capture a moral meaning in an intriguing and memorable way. Writers as diverse as Aeschylus, Francis Bacon, Samuel Butler, Euripides, Benjamin Franklin, George Herbert, Andrew Lang, James Russell Lowell, Sophocles, Jonathan Swift, Mark Twain, and Oscar Wilde have fashioned quips from Aesop's fables and adopted his style in their work. The folklore and fairy tales of Charles Perrault, the Brothers Grimm, and Hans Christian Andersen find their roots in the storytelling modes Aesop employed. So ubiquitous is Aesop's influence that countless fables are attributed to him regardless of their actual authorship. Indeed, invoking Aesop's name has become the most convenient way to describe the entire genre of the fable.

Following are some of Aesop's expressions that have entered into not only our speech but our very ways of thinking (see also *From the Pages of* Aesop's Fables, on the first page inside the front cover):

All that glitters is not gold

Blow hot and cold

Cry wolf

Dog in the manger

Every man for himself

Familiarity breeds contempt

Kill the goose that lays the golden eggs

Leave well enough alone

Lion's share

Look before you leap

Might makes right

Slow but sure

Sour grapes

Throw to the wolves

Viper in one's bosom

Wolf in sheep's clothing

# COMMENTS & QUESTIONS

*In this section, we aim to provide the reader with an array of perspectives on the text, as well as questions that challenge those perspectives. The commentary has been culled from sources as diverse as reviews contemporaneous with the work, letters written by the author, literary criticism of later generations, and appreciations written throughout history. Following the commentary, a series of questions seeks to filter Aesop's Fables through a variety of points of view and bring about a richer understanding of these enduring fables.*

## Comments

**HERODOTUS**

When the people of Delphi repeatedly made proclamation in accordance with an oracle, to find some one who would take up the blood-money for the death of Esop, no one else appeared, but at length the grandson of Iadmon, called Iadmon also, took it up; and thus it is shown that Esop . . . was the slave of Iadmon.

—from *The History of Herodotus*,
as translated by G. C. Macaulay (1890)

**OSCAR FAY ADAMS**

Teaching by fable is the most ancient method of moral instruction; and allusions to it abound in the early history of all nations. The dullest minds could be reached by an apologue or a parable, and the brightest ones were not offended by this indirect mode of giving advice. Indeed, the fable seems to have been at one period the universal method of appeal to the reason or the conscience. Kings on their thrones were addressed in fables by their courtiers and subjects were admonished by monarchs by means of skillfully-told apologues.

—from *Dear Old Story-Tellers* (1889)

**THE TIMES OF LONDON**
In England "Æsop" has remained one of the most universal of school books, and all attempts to imitate or rival him have ended in ignominious failure.

—March 21, 1890

**THE NATION**
Originally a part of folk-lore, the fable became literature in Greece because it was made the medium of conveying political lessons at a time when, under the Tyrants, free speech was dangerous. In India the same result was produced by the use of fables by the founder of Buddhism to impart moral lessons. In Greece this use is connected with the name of Æsop, about whom so little is known that it has been suggested that he is himself a fable.

—July 31, 1890

**CHARLES W. ELIOT**
In [*Aesop's Fables*], the form of the old animistic story is used without any belief in the identity of the personalities of men and animals, but with a conscious double meaning and for the purpose of teaching a lesson. The fable is a product not of the folk but of the learned; and though at times it has been handed down by word of mouth, it is really a literary form.

—from *The Harvard Classics: Folk-lore and Fable* (1909)

### Questions

1. Sometimes two proverbs contradict each other, as in "Look before you leap" and "He who hesitates is lost." When two fables (or proverbs) contradict each other must we assume that one is wrong? Can you think of two of Aesop's fables that contradict each other, although both seem to apply? Is it that both apply, but to different circumstances? If so, can you describe the circumstances?

2. Can you think of a public figure who characteristically acts moral in accordance with one of Aesop's fables?

3. Do any of these fables always apply?

4. Can one extract a worldview that governs all of these fables, rational, religious, commonsensical, or based on experience?

5. Do you think these fables, or stories, are more effective in making a point than reasoned argument would be? Why or why not?

# FOR FURTHER READING

### The Life of Aesop

*Aesop: Fables.* 1692. Translation by Sir Roger L'Estrange. Everyman's Library series. New York: Alfred A. Knopf, 1992. Includes "The Life of Aesop" (pp. 17–45).

Daly, Lloyd W. *Aesop without Morals: The Famous Fables, and a Life of Aesop.* New York: Thomas Yoseloff, 1961.

### The Aesopic Fable

Blackham, H. J. *The Fable as Literature.* London: Athlone Press, 1985.

Holzberg, Niklas. *The Ancient Fable: An Introduction.* Translated by Christine Jackson-Holzberg (from *Die antike Fabel: eine Einführung* [2001], expanded edition of an introduction to Greek and Latin fables published in 1993). Studies in Ancient Folklore and Popular Culture series. Bloomington: Indiana University Press, 2002.

Jacobs, Joseph. 1889. *History of the Aesopic Fable.* New York: Burt Franklin, 1970.

Patterson, Annabel M. *Fables of Power: Aesopian Writing and Political History.* Durham, NC: Duke University Press, 1991.

Perry, Ben Edwin. *Babrius and Phaedrus.* Newly edited and translated into English together with a historical introduction and a comprehensive survey of Greek and Latin fables in the Aesopic tradition. Loeb Classical Library series. Cambridge, MA: Harvard University Press, 1965.

## Oriental Fables

*The Jataka; or, Stories of the Buddha's Former Births.* Edited by E. B. Cowell. Cambridge: Cambridge University Press, 1895–1907. 6 vols. Reprint: Delhi: Motilal Banarsidass Publishers, 1999.

*The Panchatantra.* 1925. Translated from the Sanskrit by Arthur W. Ryder. Chicago: University of Chicago Press, 1964.

## Folktale Studies

Aarne, Antti, and Thompson, Stith. *The Types of the Folktale: A Classification and Bibliography.* Helsinki: Suomalainen Tiedeakatemia, 1961.

Ashliman, D. L. *A Guide to Folktales in the English Language.* Bibliographies and Indexes in World Literature series. Westport, CT: Greenwood Press, 1987.

Thompson, Stith. 1946. *The Folktale.* Berkeley: University of California Press, 1977. Still the best introduction to the folktale.

## Internet Resources

Ashliman, D. L. *Folktexts.* An electronic library of folktales, folklore, fairy tales, and mythology, sponsored by the University of Pittsburgh (http://www.pitt.edu/~dash/folktexts.html).

Gibbs, Laura. *Aesopica.net.* An ongoing venture, sponsored by the University of Oklahoma, to publish electronic versions of the Greek and Latin texts of Aesop's fables, together with English translations and indexes (http://liaisons.ou.edu/~lgibbs/aesopica/index.htm).

University of Southern Mississippi. *Description of the de Grummond Children's Literature Collection.* This collection is especially strong in its holdings of Aesop and other fabulists (http://www.lib.usm.edu/~degrum/html/collectionhl/ch-fables.shtml).

# ALPHABETICAL INDEX OF FABLES

## A

## B

## C

# D

# E

# F

## G

## N

## O

# P

# Q

# R

# S

## T

## V

# W